The Maverick's Secret Baby

TERI WILSON

MILLS & BOON

First published in Great Britain 2019
by Mills & Boon, an imprint of HarperCollins*Publishers*
1 London Bridge Street, London, SE1 9GF

Large Print edition 2019

© 2019 Harlequin Books S.A.

ISBN: 978-0-263-08352-1

MIX
Paper from
responsible sources
FSC™ C007454

This book is produced from independently certified FSC™ paper to ensure responsible forest management. For more information visit www.harpercollins.co.uk/green.

Printed and bound in Great Britain
by CPI Group (UK) Ltd, Croydon, CR0 4YY

Teri Wilson is a novelist for Mills & Boon. She is the author of *Unleashing Mr Darcy*, now a Hallmark Channel Original Movie. Teri is also a contributing writer at hellogiggles.com, a lifestyle and entertainment website founded by Zooey Deschanel that is now part of the *People* magazine, *Time* magazine and *Entertainment Weekly* family. Teri loves books, travel, animals and dancing every day. Visit Teri at teriwilson.net or on Twitter, @teriwilsonauthr.

This book is dedicated to my writing
friends from the Leakey, Texas,
writing retreat. From the small-town
shop with the meat cleaver door
handles to the house on the river
and the nighttime campfires,
it was the perfect inspiration
for writing a Montana romance
with a cowboy hero. I love you all.

Chapter One

Finn Crawford was living the dream.

Granted, his father, Maximilian, had gone a little crazy. The old man was intent on paying a matchmaker to marry off all six of his sons. If that wasn't nuts, Finn didn't know what was.

This wasn't the 1800s. It was modern-day Montana, and the Crawfords were... *comfortable*. If that sounded like something a rich man might say about his family, then it was probably because it was true. Finn's family was indeed wealthy, and Finn himself wasn't exactly terrible-looking. Quite the opposite, if the women who'd been ringing Viv Dalton—the matchmaker in question—were to be believed. More important, he was a decent guy. He tried, anyway.

Plus, Finn loved women. Women were typically much more open than men. Kinder and more authentic. He loved their softness and the way they committed so much to everything, whether it was caring for a stray puppy or running a business. Show him a woman who wore a deep red lipstick and her heart on her sleeve, and he was a goner. At the ripe old age of twenty-nine, Finn had already fallen in love more times than he could count.

So the very notion that he'd need any help in the marriage department would have been completely laughable, if he'd had any intention of tying the knot. Which he did *not*.

Why would he, when Viv Dalton was being paid to toss women in his direction? His dad had picked up the entire Crawford ranch—all six of his sons and over a thousand head of cattle—and moved them from Dallas to Rust Creek Falls, Montana, for this asinine pretend version of *The Bachelor.* The way Finn saw it, he'd be a fool not to enjoy the ride.

And enjoying it, he had been. A little too much, according to Viv.

"Finn, honestly. You've dated a different woman nearly every week for the past three months." The wedding planner eyed him from across her desk, which was piled high with bridal magazines and puffy white tulle. Sitting inside her wedding shop was like being in the middle of a cupcake.

"And they've all been lovely." Finn stretched his denim-clad legs out in front of him and crossed his cowboy boots at the ankle. "I have zero complaints."

Beside him, Maximilian sighed. "I have a lot of complaints. Specifically, a million of them where you're concerned, son."

Finn let the words roll right off him. After all, paying someone a million dollars to find wives for all six Crawford brothers hadn't been his genius idea. Maximilian had no one to blame but himself.

"Mr. Crawford, I assure you I'm doing my best to find Finn a bride." Viv tucked a wayward strand of blond hair behind her ear and folded her hands neatly on the surface of her desk. All business. "In fact, I believe I've set him up with every eligible woman in Rust Creek Falls."

"All of them?" Finn arched a brow. This town was even smaller than he'd thought it was. It would have taken him a lifetime to go through the entire dating pool back in Dallas. He should know— he'd tried.

Vivienne gave him a tight smile. "Every. Last. One."

"Okay, then I guess we're done here. You gave it your best shot." Finn stood. He'd miss the girlfriend-of-the-week club, but at least his father would be forced to accept the fact that he wasn't about to get engaged to any of the fine female residents of Rust Creek Falls.

Finn placed his Stetson on his head, set to go. "Thank you, ma'am."

"Sit back down, son." Maximilian didn't raise his voice, but his tone had an edge to it that Finn hadn't heard since the time he'd "borrowed" his father's truck to go mudding with his high school buddies back in tenth grade.

That little escapade had ended with Maximilian's luxury F-150 stuck in a ditch and Finn mucking out stalls every weekend for the rest of the school year.

Of course Finn was an adult now, not a stupid teenager. He made his own choices, certainly when it came to his love life. But he loved his dad, and since the Crawfords were all business partners in addition to family, he didn't want to rock the boat. Not over something as ridiculous as this.

"Sure thing, Dad." He lowered himself back into the frilly white chair with its frilly lace cushion.

Maximilian sat a little straighter and narrowed his gaze at Viv Dalton. "Are you forgetting what's at stake?"

She cleared her throat. "No, sir. I'm not."

A look of warning passed from Finn's father toward the wedding planner, and she gave him a tiny, almost imperceptible nod.

Finn's gut churned. What the hell was that about?

Damn it.

Knowing his dad, he'd gone and upped the ante behind Finn's back. When Maximilian ran into problems, he had a tendency to write a bigger check to make them go away.

Finn sighed. "I'm no longer sure entirely what's going on here, but I think it might be time for this little matchmaking project to end. Half of us are already married."

One by one, Finn's brothers Logan, Xander and Knox had become attached. It was uncanny, really. None of them had ended up with women of Viv's choosing, but they'd coupled up all the same. The way he saw it, his dad should be thrilled. The Crawford legacy would live on, Finn's bachelor status notwithstanding.

Maximilian shook his head. "Absolutely not. We need Viv's help now more than ever. It's not going to be easy to make matches for you, Hunter and Wilder. Hunter hasn't so much as looked at another woman since his wife died. Wilder is just…well, Wilder. And you can't seem to focus on one woman to save your life. If you're not careful, son, you're going to wind up old, alone and lonely. Just like me."

A bark of laugher escaped Finn before he could stop it.

"Please." He rolled his eyes. "You're far from lonely."

His father was rarely, if ever, alone. The business and living arrangements at their sprawling Ambling A Ranch pretty much assured that Maximilian saw each of his six sons on a daily basis. Plus, he was the biggest flirt Finn had ever set eyes on.

His dad had been single for decades. Finn's mother had abandoned the family when all six of her sons had been young. Maximilian might have remained single, but that hardly meant he lacked female companionship. His wallet alone was an aphrodisiac—plus he was something of a silver fox. Being in his sixties didn't stop him from dating nearly as much as Finn did.

Like father, like son.

"Point taken." Maximilian shrugged one shoulder. The corner of his mouth inched up into a half grin. "In any case, we're not here to talk about me. We're here to find you a bride."

"Your son might need to adjust his standards," Viv said, as if Finn wasn't sitting right there in the room. "The sheer number of women he's dated in the past three months should have guaranteed a good match."

"I guess you'll just have to dredge up more women. It seems like the only solution." Finn aimed his best sardonic smile directly at the wedding planner. She was really beginning to annoy him.

Adjust his standards? What the hell was that supposed to mean?

"I've been calling around town to see if I've overlooked any single ladies. This morning alone I've tried all the day-care centers, the veterinary clinic, the medical center and Maverick Manor." Viv tapped a polished fingernail on the pink note-pad in front of her. "I thought maybe I could find a few datable, single women working in one of these locations whom I might not be acquainted with, some ladies living in one of the surrounding counties."

So now she was going to import women into town to date him? This whole ordeal was getting more absurd by the minute.

"Any luck?" Maximilian said.

"Not yet. But there's still one place left on my list—Strickland's Boarding House."

An ache took up residence in Finn's temples. "That ramshackle Victorian mansion by the fire station?"

Viv's lips pursed. "It's a town land-mark."

"It's purple," Finn retorted.

"Lavender gray, technically." She smiled

brightly at him. Jeez, this woman never gave up, did she? *Maybe because your father is offering her a million dollars to marry you off...possibly more.* "Just the sort of place a lovely single woman might choose to stay."

"That actually makes sense, son." Maximilian waved a hand toward Viv's list. "Go ahead and call over to the boarding house. We'll wait."

Finn was on the verge of pulling his Stetson low over his eyes and taking a nap. No one here seemed to care much what he thought, anyway. But once Viv dialed the number, she put her phone on speaker mode, which made napping pretty much impossible.

After two rings, an older man's voice rattled on the other end. "Howdy, Strickland's Boarding House."

Viv smiled. "Hello there, Gene. It's Vivienne Dalton calling."

"Hi there, darlin'. What can Melba and I do for you today?" he said.

In the background, Finn heard a woman—Melba, presumably—asking who'd called. When Old Gene supplied her with the information, she yelled out a greeting to Viv.

Viv and Old Gene exchanged a few more pleasantries. Gene asked about her husband, and she inquired as to the well-being of the baby pygmy goat Gene and Melba were caring for.

Of course there's a baby pygmy goat. Finn suppressed a grin. Maximilian, however, was less charmed. He cleared his throat, prompting Viv to get on with the matter at hand.

She took the hint. "Actually, Gene, I have a rather odd question for you. Do you happen to have any single young women staying at the boarding house who might be interested in a date with a handsome cowboy named Finn Crawford? I'm trying to help out a friend who's new in town."

"Funny you should mention single

young women," Old Gene said. "We've had a darling young lady staying with us for a couple weeks now. A bit on the shy side, but sweet as pie."

Viv's eyes lit up. "Really? What's her name?"

"Avery."

Finn narrowed his gaze at Viv's phone. *Avery?*

The only Avery he knew would never fit into a place like Rust Creek Falls. She couldn't possibly be talking about…

"Avery who?" Maximilian growled. "Please tell me you're not talking about the daughter of that rat bas—"

"Dad." Finn shook his head. "Chill out."

As usual, Maximilian had a harsh word at the ready for anyone related to his old nemesis, Oscar Ellington.

Finn was certain he didn't need to worry. It just wasn't possible. Oscar Ellington's daughter lived over a thousand miles away, in Texas. Plus, with her pencil skirts, red-soled stilettos and designer handbags, she wasn't exactly what Finn would describe as sweet. Considering they'd only shared one night together, she wasn't exactly *his*, either.

Still, what a night it had been.

"Gene! Stop talking right this minute!" Melba's voice boomed in the background again.

Viv frowned down at her phone. "Is everything okay over there?"

"Fine and dandy," Gene said.

Melba issued a simultaneous "No, it is not. Gene seems to have forgotten we shouldn't be giving out guests' private information."

"But she seems a little lonely," Old Gene countered while Melba continued to balk.

Again, Finn's memory snagged on a sweet, sultry night on an Oklahoma business trip and the most electric kiss he'd ever experienced. The power had gone down, bathing the city in darkness. But when his lips touched Avery Ellington's, they'd created enough sparks to light up the sky.

How long had it been?

Months.

"Excuse me." Finn leaned forward in his chair. He knew he was supposed to be a quiet observer at the moment, but he had to ask. "What exactly does this Avery woman look like?"

The glare Viv aimed his way shot daggers at him.

"Never mind," she said primly. "Sorry to bother you, Gene. We'll chat soon. Give that baby goat a kiss for me. Bye now."

She ended the call, and for a minute, Finn was seriously worried she might throw the phone at his head. "What does she *look like*? You can't be serious."

Maximilian shrugged. "It's a legitimate question."

Finn held up a hand. "Wait. That's not what—"

But Viv wasn't having it. She cut him off before he could explain. "There are far more important things than looks when it comes to a potential life partner."

Agreed.

Finn wasn't looking for a life partner, though. He doubted he'd be looking for one for another decade or so. Besides, he'd simply been trying to figure out if they'd been talking about the same Avery. All Old Gene needed to say was long, lush brown hair and dark, expressive eyes. Then he would have known.

Give it up. This is the opposite end of the country from Texas.

Or Oklahoma, for that matter.

Besides, Avery Ellington would stick out like a sore thumb in Rust Creek Falls. Surely he'd have run into her by now.

"You've found all of Viv's picks attractive so far, son. I'm sure this Avery girl wouldn't be any different," Maximilian said.

Finn let out a long exhale. How shallow could his father possibly make him sound? Maybe it was time to stop humoring the old man and dating every woman Viv Dalton threw at him.

"Thank you for everything, Ms. Dalton, but I think it's time to go." Finn stood and turned toward Maximilian. "Dad?"

His father didn't budge.

Fine. He could waste all the time and money he desired, but Finn was out of there. He tipped his hat to Viv and waded through all the pastel cupcake fluff toward the exit. All the while, his father's words echoed in his head.

I'm sure this Avery girl wouldn't be any different.

That's where he was wrong.

Finn had never met a woman quite like Avery Ellington.

* * *

Avery Ellington tucked her yoga mat under her arm and made her way down the curved staircase of the old Victorian house where she'd been living for the past few weeks.

Living? Ha. Hiding is more like it.

Her grip on the banister tightened. She didn't want to dwell on her reasons for tucking herself away at Strickland's Boarding House in Nowheresville, Montana. She had more pressing problems at the moment—like the fact that her Lululemons were practically bursting at the seams.

Even so, instead of heading to the back porch for her early-morning yoga session when she reached the foot of the stairs, she veered toward the kitchen to see what smelled so good in there.

Her appetite had never been so active back in Dallas. She hardly recognized herself. Before, breakfast consisted of a skinny triple latte consumed en route to a business meeting. Then again, her entire life had been different *before*. This new *after* was strange…different.

And scary as heck.

"Ah, good morning, dear." Melba wiped her hands on her apron and smiled as Avery entered the boarding house's huge kitchen. "Claire just left to take Bekkah to school, but she made a fresh batch of muffins earlier. Would you like some?"

Claire, the Stricklands' granddaughter, was the official cook for the boarding house. She and her family used to live with the Stricklands, but according to Old Gene, they'd recently moved out, leaving Melba a little out of sorts. Claire still came by regularly to cook, but Melba's empty nest meant Avery got more than her fair share of the older woman's attention.

Not that being doted on was a bad thing, necessarily. Truth be told, Avery was accustomed to it. She'd been doted on her entire life.

"Good morning. And thank you." Avery bit into a muffin and nodded toward her mat. "I'm about to do a little yoga out back. It's such a nice, crisp day."

God, who was she? She sounded like Gwyneth Paltrow on a spa weekend instead of the Avery Ellington she'd been since graduating with honors from the University of Texas and stepping up as the vice president of Ellington Meats.

You're still the same person. This is only temporary. Mostly, anyway.

Right. As soon as she did what she'd come to Rust Creek Falls to do, she'd go straight home and get back to her regular life in Dallas. Her *charmed* life. The life that she loved.

"Here you go." Melba handed her a steaming mug of something that smelled wonderful—nutmeg, brown sugar and warm apple pie. Autumn in a cup.

"We've had hot apple cider simmering all morning. This will get you nice and warmed up before you go outside."

"Thank you." Avery took a deep inhale of the fragrant cider and had a sudden urge to curl up and knit by the fire in the boarding house's cozy hearth instead of practicing her downward dog.

Never mind that she'd never held a knitting needle in her life. Clearly she'd been in Montana too long.

She took a sip and glanced at Old Gene, sitting at the kitchen table with a live goat in his lap. "How's the baby this morning?"

Baby.

Her throat went dry, and she took another gulp of cider.

"She's settling in." Old Gene nodded and offered the adorable animal a large baby bottle. The goat wasted no time latching on.

Melba rolled her eyes. "If you call waking up every two hours 'settling in.' Honestly, I don't know what possessed you to bring that thing home."

"My cousin is in the hospital with a broken hip, and he's got a barn full of animals that need tending. What was I supposed to do? Bring home a pig?"

Melba tossed a handful of cinnamon sticks into the pot of cider. "Lord, help me."

Old Gene winked at Avery behind Melba's back, and she smiled into her mug. The morning goat wars had become a regular thing since Gene had returned from his rescue mission to his cousin's farm a week or so ago, goat in hand. Melba was antigoat, particularly indoors, whereas Old Gene doted on the animal like it was a child.

Avery had yet to go anywhere near it. She didn't know a thing about goats. Or baby bottles, for that matter.

"You're really doing your best to get

on my last nerve this morning." Melba sighed.

"I was simply trying to do something nice," Old Gene muttered. "You never know. Avery might enjoy going on a date with a nice young man."

"Wait…what?" She blinked.

How had the conversation moved seamlessly and at lightning speed from the goat to her love life?

"Gene." Melba looked like she might hit him over the head with her ladle.

"Can I ask what you two are talking about?" Avery set her mug down on the counter with a *thunk*.

Old Gene shrugged. "Viv Dalton just called. Apparently she knows a lonely cowboy."

"Don't you worry, dear." Melba reached for her hand and gave it a pat. "I made sure Viv knows you're not interested in meeting a man right now. Old Gene had no business even giving her your name."

Avery had no idea who Viv Dalton was, nor did she care. But she cared *very much* about her name floating around town. She might be new to Rust Creek Falls, but she was well aware of how swiftly the rumor mill worked. Case in point: Melba knew her husband was bringing home a goat before he'd even walked through the door. Old Gene had stopped by the general store for supplies on the way back to the boarding house and before his truck had pulled into the driveway, Melba had already gotten half a dozen texts and calls about the furry little kid.

"You gave my name to a stranger?" Avery felt sick.

The goat let loose with a pitiful bleat that perfectly mirrored the panic swirling in her consciousness.

Old Gene and Melba exchanged a worried glance.

"Only your first name." Melba reached

for Avery's empty cup and refilled it with another ladleful of fragrant apple cider. A peace offering. "I'm sorry, dear. Old Gene was just trying to help, but I set him straight."

Avery nodded.

She wasn't sure what to say at this point. The day she arrived, she'd made it very clear to Melba that she was in town for a little respite. She'd been in desperate need of peace and quiet.

Avery had a feeling Melba assumed she was on the run from a bad boyfriend—maybe even a not-so-nice husband. She was somewhat ashamed to admit that she'd done nothing to correct this assumption. But it had been the only way to prevent her arrival in Rust Creek Falls from hitting the rumor circuit.

Her time had run out, apparently.

"Apologize to Avery, Gene." Melba pointed at her husband with a wooden spoon.

"I'm sorry," he said.

Avery smiled in return, because it was impossible to be angry at a man bottle-feeding a baby goat. "You're forgiven."

Melba let out a relieved exhale and turned back to the stove. "Go on now and do your yoga in peace. Gene and I both know you're not one bit interested in meeting that Crawford boy, no matter how charming and handsome Viv Dalton says he is."

Avery almost dropped her yoga mat.

That Crawford boy?

She couldn't be talking about Finn. Absolutely not.

Please, please no.

And yet somehow she knew it was true.

Charming? Check.

Handsome? Double check.

She swallowed hard, but bile rose up the back of her throat before she could stop it. She felt like she might be sick to her stomach…again. But that was pretty much par for the course now, just like her crazy new insatiable food cravings and the broken zipper on her favorite pencil skirt.

The goat slurped at the baby bottle, and Avery stared at the tiny animal. So utterly helpless. So sweet.

Tears pricked her eyes, and she blinked them away.

Get a grip.

She had more important things to dwell on than an orphaned goat. *Far* more important, like how on earth she could possibly explain to Melba and Old Gene that the last thing she wanted was to be set up with Finn Crawford when she was already four months pregnant with his child.

Chapter Two

No amount of downward dogs could calm the frantic beating of Avery's heart. She tried. She really did. But after an hour on her yoga mat, she felt more unsettled than ever.

Probably because every time she closed her eyes, she saw Finn Crawford's handsome face and his tilted, cocky smirk that never failed to make her weak in the knees.

She huffed out a distinctly nonyogi breath, scrambled to her feet and rolled up her mat. So much for the quiet, peaceful space she'd managed to carve out for herself in Rust Creek Falls. Her little time-out was over. She could no longer ignore the fact that she'd come here to find her baby's father—not when fate had nearly thrown her right back into his path.

"Finished already, dear?" Melba said when Avery pushed through the screen door and back into the kitchen of the boarding house. She shook her head. "I don't understand why you young girls enjoy twisting yourselves into pretzels."

Melba's apron was dotted with flour, and a fresh platter of homemade biscuits sat on the kitchen island. The baby goat snoozed quietly on a dog bed in the corner by the window.

"Yes. I think I'm getting a little stir-crazy." She needed a nice distraction, something to completely rid her mind of Finn Crawford until she worked out exactly how to tell him he was going to be a daddy. "Maybe I could help clean some of the guest rooms again?"

Back home in Dallas, Avery typically put in a sixty-hour workweek. Fifty, minimum. She couldn't remember having so much free time on her hands. *Ever.* When she'd first arrived in Montana, all the unprecedented free time had been a dream come true. Pregnancy hormones had been wreaking havoc on her work schedule. The day before she'd left town, she'd actually nodded off in the middle of a marketing meeting. She'd needed a respite. A work cleanse.

Staying at the boarding house had given her just that. And it was lovely...

Until the morning she couldn't force the zipper closed on her favorite jeans—the boyfriend-cut ones that were always so soft and baggy. Faced with such painful evidence of the life growing inside her, Avery had experienced a sudden longing for her old life. She didn't know the first thing about babies or being pregnant, so she'd thrown herself into helping out around the boarding house in an effort to rid herself of her anxiety. Unfortunately, she knew as much about cleaning as she knew about caring for an infant.

"Oh. Well. That's certainly a kind offer." Melba picked up a dishcloth and scrubbed at an invisible spot on the counter. "But I'm not sure that's such a good idea. Old Gene is upstairs, still trying to unclog the toilet in the big corner room."

Avery's face bloomed with heat. The clogged toilet had been her doing. But what were the odds she'd accidentally flush another sponge?

The baby goat let out a long, warbly bleat. *Meeeeeeehhhhhhhh.*

Avery narrowed her gaze at its little ginger head. Was the animal taunting her now?

Melba cleared her throat. "Don't look so sad, dear. If you really want to help out around here, I'm sure we can figure something out."

"I do. Honestly, I'll try anything." Except maybe bottle-feeding the goat. That was a hard no.

Melba consulted the to-do list tacked to the refrigerator with a Fall Mountain magnet. "I need to make a run to the general store. Would you like to come along?"

Avery's heart gave a little leap. She was much better at shopping than cleaning toilets. She *excelled* at it, quite frankly. A closetful of Louboutins didn't lie. "Shopping? Yes, count me in."

"You're sure?" Melba gave her one of the gentle, sympathetic glances that had convinced Avery the older woman thought she was running from some kind of danger. "You haven't wanted to get out much."

Avery nodded. She was going to have to leave the boarding house at some point. Besides, the odds of running into

Finn Crawford or his notorious father at the general store were zero. Not a chance. They weren't the sort of men who ran errands. They had employees for that kind of thing. How else would Finn have time to wine and dine every eligible woman in town?

"We're just going to the general store, right? Nowhere else? I have a…um… conference call later, so I shouldn't stay out too long." There was no conference call. At least not that Avery knew of. She hadn't checked in to the office for days. Another first.

If she called in, her father would surely pick up the phone. She'd been a daddy's girl all her life, through and through. That would change once he found out she was carrying Finn's baby. Oscar Ellington would rather she have a child with the devil himself.

"Straight to the general store and back." Melba made a cross-my-heart gesture with her fingertips over the pinafore of her apron.

"Super! I'll run upstairs and change." Avery beamed and scurried up to her corner room on the third floor of the rambling mansion.

Along the way, she heard Old Gene cursing at the clogged toilet, and she winced. The wincing continued as she tried—and failed—to find something presentable that she could still manage to zip or button at the waist.

It was no use—she was going to have to stick with her yoga pants and slip into the oversize light blue button-down shirt she'd borrowed from Old Gene. Lovely. If by some strange twist of fate Finn did turn up at the general store, he probably wouldn't even recognize her.

Any lingering worries she had about running into him were instantly kicked into high gear when she and Melba reached the redbrick building on the corner of Main and Cedar Streets. Melba said something about the amber and gold autumnal window display, but Avery couldn't form a response. She was too busy gaping at the sign above the front door.

Crawford's General Store.

Did Finn's family *own* this place?

"Avery?" Melba rested gentle fingertips on her forearm. "Are you okay?"

"Yes. Yes, of course." She pasted on a smile. "I just noticed the name of the store—Crawford's. Does it belong to the family you mentioned earlier?"

"Heavens, no. The general store has been here for generations. The Montana Crawfords have lived in Rust Creek Falls for as long as I can remember. The new family is from Texas."

I'm aware.

Seriously, though. Finn's family was huge, and Rust Creek Falls was very small. Quaint and cozy, but rural in every way. Their addition to the population must mean that half the town had the same last name all of a sudden.

"I see," Avery said.

She tore her gaze away from the store's signage long enough to finally take in the window display, with its garland of oak and maple leaves and towering pile of pumpkins. They'd walked a grand total of two blocks, and already she'd seen enough hay bales, woven baskets and gourds to make her wonder if the entire town was drunk on pumpkin spice lattes.

Autumn wasn't such a big thing in Texas. The warm weather back home meant no apple picking, no fall foliage and definitely no need for snuggly oversize sweaters. It was kind of a shame, really.

But here in Montana, fall was ushered in with a lovely and luminous harvest moon, smoky breezes that smelled of wood fire and the crunch of leaves underfoot. Avery had never experienced anything like it.

"Maybe we should get some ingredients for caramel apples and make them for my great-granddaughter Bekkah's kindergarten class. I always bring some to the big Halloween dance, but the children might like an early taste." Melba glanced over her shoulder at Avery as she pushed through the general store's entrance. "What do you think?"

"I think that's a marvelous idea." Avery had never made caramel apples before, but there was a first time for everything.

Apples...autumn...*babies*.

She glanced past the dry goods section near the front of the store and spotted a rack of flannel shirts, quilted jackets and cable-knit cardigans. It wasn't exactly Neiman Marcus, but she was going to have to bite the bullet and invest in a few things that actually fit her changing body.

"Good morning, ladies. Is there any-thing I can help you with?" A slim woman with dark wavy hair, big brown eyes and a Crawford's General Store bib apron greeted them with a wide smile.

"Yes, please." Melba pulled a lengthy shopping list out of her handbag and plopped it onto the counter. Then she ges-tured toward Avery. "Nina, I'd like you to meet Avery. She's one of our boarders."

Nina offered Avery her hand. "Wel-come to Rust Creek Falls. I'm Nina Crawford Traub."

Seriously. Did *everyone* in this town have the same last name?

"Hello." Avery shook Nina's hand, then dashed off to grab a few warm, roomy items of clothing while the other women tackled Melba's list of supplies.

By the time she returned, the counter was piled high. It looked like Melba was buying out the entire store.

"Wow." Avery's eye widened. She

clutched her new flannels close to her chest, because there wasn't enough space to set them down. "This is…"

"Impressive," someone behind her said. There was a smile in his voice, a delicious drawl that Avery felt deep in the pit of her stomach. "Here's hoping you've left some stuff for the rest of us."

Don't turn around, her thoughts screamed. She knew that voice. It was as velvety smooth as hot buttered rum and oh, so familiar.

But just like the last time she'd been in the same room with the bearer of that soulful Texas accent, her body reacted before her brain could kick into gear. Sure enough, when she spun around, she found herself face-to-face with the very man she so desperately needed to speak to—Finn Crawford, the father-to-be, looking hotter than ever wearing a black Stetson and an utterly shocked expression on his handsome face.

Avery realized a second too late what was about to happen. Trouble.

So.

Very.

Much.

Trouble.

Avery?

Finn blinked. Hard.

No way... No possible way.

He was hallucinating. Or more likely, simply mistaken. After all, the brunette beauty who'd just spun around to stare at him might bear more than a passing resemblance to Avery Ellington, but she was hugging a stack of flannel shirts like it was some kind of security blanket. The Avery he knew wouldn't be caught dead in plaid flannel. She might even be allergic to it.

It had to be her, though. On some visceral level, he just *knew*. Plus he'd recognize those big doe eyes anywhere.

Avery Ellington. Warmth filled his chest. *Well, isn't this a fine surprise.*

Finn glanced at the older woman beside her—Melba… Melba *Strickland*, as in the owner of Strickland's Boarding House. So Old Gene's "darling young lady" that Viv Dalton wanted to set him up with was indeed the Avery he knew so well.

He burst out laughing.

Avery's soft brown eyes narrowed. She looked like she might be contemplating dropping the flannel and using her hands to strangle him. "What's so funny?"

"This." He gestured back and forth between Avery and Melba. "I'm not sure you're aware, but an hour or so ago, we were almost set up on a blind date."

"I might have heard something about that," Avery said, clearly failing to find the humor in the situation.

She seemed a little rattled. If Finn didn't know better, he would have thought she was unhappy to run into him. But that couldn't be right. The last time they'd seen one another had been immensely pleasurable.

For both of them.

Finn was certain of it. Plus, they'd parted on good terms.

"It's incredibly good to see you. What on earth are you doing in Rust Creek Falls?" He arched a brow. She was awfully far away from her daddy's ranch in Texas.

Melba interjected before Avery could respond, "Avery is a guest at the boarding house."

Finn nodded, even though they'd already covered Avery's local living arrangements. It still didn't explain what she was doing clear across the country from home.

He swiveled his gaze back to Avery. She looked beautiful, but different somehow. He couldn't quite put his finger on what had changed. Maybe it was the casual clothes or her wind-tossed hair, but her usual cool elegance had been replaced with a warmth that made him acutely aware of his own heartbeat all of a sudden.

"How's the little one?" he said with a smile.

"Um." Avery blinked like an owl. "How did you—"

Finn shrugged. "Everyone in town is talking about it. There's nothing quite as cute as a baby goat."

"The goat. Right." Avery swallowed, and he traced the movement up and down the graceful column of her throat.

Was it his imagination, or did she seem nervous?

"The goat's cute, but she's a handful. I don't know what Old Gene was thinking." Melba rolled her eyes. "She has to be bottle-fed every four to five hours, round the clock. It's almost like having a real baby again, but maybe a little less noisy."

Avery turned toward Melba with an incredulous stare. "*Less* noisy?"

Melba shrugged. "Sure. You know how babies are."

Avery shifted from one foot to the other as she glanced at Finn and then quickly looked away.

Melba's eyes narrowed. "How exactly do you two know each other?"

Why did the question feel like a test of some sort?

Finn gave her an easy smile. He had nothing to hide. "Avery and I are both in the beef business."

"Really?" Melba looked him and up down.

"Absolutely. Our paths used to cross every so often, but we haven't bumped into each other since my family relocated to Montana." A pity, really. "I'd love to take you out while you're in town, Avery."

She bit the swell of her lush bottom lip. "Oh…um, well…"

Not exactly the reaction he was going for. Avery looked as scared as a rabbit, and Melba was once again scrutinizing him as if he were giving off serial killer vibes.

Was he missing something?

His thoughts drifted back to the night they'd spent together in Oklahoma City. It didn't take much effort. The entire encounter was seared in his memory— every perfect, porcelain inch of Avery's skin, every tender brush of her lips.

They'd been in town for a gala dinner of cattle executives, and Finn would be lying if he'd said he hadn't been hoping to run into her. Through their overlapping business connections and a handful of mutual friends, Finn and Avery had been moving in the same orbit for quite a few years. He'd wanted her for every single one of them. How could he not? She was lovely. And smart, too. It took a special kind of woman to hold her own as the vice president of a major company in a business dominated by men. Finn considered himself a Southern gentleman, but that wasn't true of everyone in the beef business. Avery had run into her fair share of chauvinists and good old boys, but she never failed to rise above their nonsense with her head held high.

As much as she fascinated him, he'd respected her too much to make a real move. Their interactions had been limited to a low-key flirtation that he found immensely enjoyable, if somewhat torturous.

But the night in Oklahoma had been different. June in the Sooner State was always a nightmare of blazing heat and suffocating humidity, but that particular weekend had been especially brutal. A heat wave swept through the area, causing widespread power outages as the temperature soared. The gala's luxury hotel was plunged into darkness. Even after they got the generator up and running, the crystal chandeliers were barely illuminated, and heady, scented candles were scattered over every available surface.

He remembered Avery saying something about the animosity between their families, and true, his father had never uttered a kind word about Oscar Ellington. Quite the opposite, actually. There was definitely bad blood between the Crawford and Ellington patriarchs. But Finn and Avery had always managed to get along. And something about the darkness made their little flirtation seem not so low-key anymore, so over laugher and dry martinis at the bar, they'd agreed to set aside any familial difficulty.

She'd looked so damned beautiful in

the candlelight, all soft curves and wide, luminous eyes. He'd taken a chance and leaned in…

He swallowed hard at the memory of what came next. It had been like something out of a dream. A perfect night—so perfect he hadn't taken another woman to bed since, despite his popularity in Montana. And now Avery was right here, less than an arm's length away, when he'd thought he'd never see her again.

"Please," he said. "Dinner, or even just coffee? For old times' sake."

He'd been neck-deep in women for the past three months, and now he was begging for an hour of Avery Ellington's time. Wonderful.

Melba cut in again before she could give him an answer. "Look at the time! Sorry to interrupt, but we simply must be going. Avery, how could you let me forget? We have to stop over at the Dalton Law Office to pick up those papers for Gene."

Avery's expression went blank. "What papers?"

"Those very important papers. You know the ones." Melba took the flannel shirts from Avery and handed them to Nina, who shoved them into a bag.

Avery crossed her arms, uncrossed them and crossed them again. Finn's gaze snagged on her oversize blue button-down. Was that a *man's* shirt she was wearing?

His jaw clenched. They hadn't even spoken since that simmering night in June, but Finn didn't like the thought of her with another man. Not one bit.

Overreacting much? It was one night, not an actual relationship. Maybe he wasn't such a fine Southern gentleman, after all.

"Come on, now. We don't want to keep Ben Dalton waiting." Melba shoved one of her five shopping bags at Avery and then linked elbows with her.

"Right. Of course we don't." Avery glanced at him one last time as Melba practically dragged her out of the store. "It was good seeing you, Finn. Goodbye."

He stared after them, wondering what in the hell had just happened.

"Can I help you find anything, Mr. Crawford?" Nina said from behind the counter.

Finn dragged his gaze away from the scene beyond the shop window and Avery's chocolate-hued hair, whipping around her angelic face in the wind like a dark halo.

He smiled, but his heart wasn't in it. "No, thank you."

For some strange reason, he almost felt like he'd already found what he needed. And now he'd just watched her walk away.

Again.

* * *

"Where are we going, exactly?" Avery gripped her shopping bag until her knuckles turned white and did her best to resist the overwhelming urge to glance over her shoulder for another glimpse of the general store.

Of Finn.

She almost wanted to believe she'd imagined their entire awkward encounter just now. Since the moment she'd first spotted the two tiny pink lines on the drugstore pregnancy test she'd taken in her posh executive washroom at Ellington Meats, she'd tried to imagine what she'd say to Finn the next time she saw him. Somehow she always imagined she'd be able to utter more than two stuttered words.

Had she managed to string a whole sentence together at all? Nope, she was pretty sure she hadn't. So much for being a strong, independent woman and facing the situation head-on.

"We're not going anywhere, dear. I thought you were going to faint when you saw Finn Crawford. I made something up to get you out of there." Melba gave her hand a comforting pat.

So her panic had been that obvious? Fabulous.

"Oh, thank you. But I was surprised, that's all." Shocked to her core was more like it.

Which was really kind of ridiculous, since the whole reason she'd come to Rust Creek Falls was to tell him about the baby. Get in, drop the baby bomb and get out. That had been the plan. It was just so much harder than she'd imagined. And now here she was, a couple weeks later, still secretly pregnant.

"Finn is an old friend." She stared straight ahead as they walked back to the boarding house. What had just transpired at the general store was a minor setback, not a total disaster. It's not like she could have told him she was pregnant right then and there.

Hey, so great to see you. FYI, I'm having your baby, and I'm planning to raise it on my own. Just wanted to let you know. I've got to pay for my pile of flannel now. Have a nice life.

Beside her, Melba snorted. "Well. He seems to have a lot of friends, if you know what I mean."

Avery's steps slowed as her heart pounded hard in her chest. "I don't, actually."

"It seems pretty obvious that you aren't ready to jump into a relationship. In any event, from what I've heard, Finn Crawford wouldn't be a great candidate."

Avery concentrated hard on putting one foot in front of the other as she turned Melba's words over in her mind. She was almost afraid to ask for more information, but she had to, didn't she? If the father of her baby was an ax murderer or something, that seemed like vital information to have. "Melba, what exactly have you heard?"

The older woman shook her head. "Don't get me wrong. He's a right charming fellow—possibly *too* charming. He's dated practically everyone in Rust Creek Falls since his family moved to town. It's sweet that he asked you to dinner, but Finn isn't right for a nice girl like you."

A nice girl like you.

What on earth would Melba think if she knew the real story?

Avery took a deep breath. The air smelled like cinnamon and nutmeg, courtesy of the decorative cinnamon brooms so many of the local business included in the fall pumpkin displays decorating the sidewalk. But the cozy atmosphere couldn't get her mind off a troubling truth—Finn might not be a serial killer, but apparently, he was a serial *flirt*. Somehow she didn't think a baby would fit neatly into a carefree lifestyle like the one Melba had just described.

But that was fine. More than fine, really. She didn't need Finn's help. If she could run the business division of a Fortune 500 company, she could certainly raise a baby. Her father would blow a gasket once he found out his first grandchild was going to be a Crawford, but he'd get over it. Having Finn out of the picture might even make things easier, where the whole family feud matter was concerned.

She obviously needed to let Finn know it was happening, though. That just seemed like the right thing to do. His reputation around Rust Creek Falls didn't change a thing. It wasn't as if she'd thought she could actually build a life with the man.

Still, the fact that he'd been acting as if Montana was the set of *Bachelor in*

Paradise while she was battling morning sickness and freaking out about starting a family with the son of her father's sworn enemy stung a little bit.

Who am I kidding? Avery climbed the steps of Strickland's Boarding House alongside Melba and thought about all the nights she'd spent in this house, secretly wishing Finn would call or text out of the blue so she'd feel less awkward about their situation. Less lonely.

It stings a lot.

Chapter Three

"Mr. Crawford." Melba Strickland stood on the front steps of her big purple house and looked Finn up and down. "This is a surprise."

Was it?

Finn got the feeling she wasn't shocked to see him in the least. The furrow in her brow told him she wasn't pleased about his impromptu visit, either.

"Good morning, Mrs. Strickland." He tipped his hat and smiled, but her frown only deepened.

Once Finn had recovered from the shock of running into Avery at the general store the day before, he'd realized she'd never given his invitation a straight answer. Granted, she hadn't exactly jumped for joy when he'd told her he wanted to take her out while she was in town, but she hadn't turned him down, either. Melba hadn't given her a chance.

After he'd finally collected what he needed at the store, he'd returned to the Ambling A and spent the afternoon making repairs to the ranch's barbed-wire fence. One of the things Finn liked best about Montana was its vast and sweeping sky. He'd always loved the deep blue of the heavens in Texas, but here it almost felt like the sky was stacked on top of itself like a layered cake. A man could do a lot of thinking under a sky like that, and while he'd pounded new fence posts into the rich red earth, he'd managed to convince himself things with Avery hadn't been as awkward as he'd imagined. Old Gene probably had papers waiting to be picked up at the Dalton Law Office, just like Melba said. There was no legitimate reason why Avery should be trying to avoid him.

Now, in the fresh light of day, he wasn't so sure. Melba was definitely giving him the side-eye as he shifted his weight from one foot to the other and tried to see past her to the inside of the boarding house.

Was she even going to let him in?

"I stopped by to see Avery." He nodded toward the bouquet in his hand—sunflowers and velvety wine-colored roses tied with a smooth satin ribbon. "And to give her these."

Melba glanced at the flowers. Her resistance wavered, ever so slightly.

"I'll have to see if Avery is available." She held up a hand. "Wait here."

"Yes, ma'am." He winced as she shut the door in his face.

Finn felt like a teenager again, trying to get permission to take a pretty girl to the school dance. Even back then, he wasn't sure he'd ever run into a protective parent as steadfast as Melba Strickland.

At long last, the door swung open to reveal Avery with her thick brunette waves piled on top of her head and her lips painted red, just like she'd looked that fateful night in Oklahoma. But instead of her usual business attire, she was wearing faded jeans and an oversize cable-knit sweater that slipped off one shoulder as she gripped the doorknob. Finn's attention snagged briefly on the flash of her smooth, bare skin, and when he met her gaze again, her mouth curved into a bashful smile.

"Finn Crawford, whatever are you doing here?" She tilted her head, and a lock of hair curled against her exposed collarbone.

It took every ounce of Finn's willpower not to reach out and wind it around his fingertips. "Shouldn't I be asking you that question?"

What *was* she doing in Montana…in Rust Creek Falls, of all places?

"I had business nearby, and since I was a bit intrigued by the charming town you'd told me all about, I thought I'd check it out while I was in the area." That's right—the last time they'd seen each other, he'd told her all about the plans to relocate the ranch. "It seemed like a nice place to escape for a few days."

Finn nodded, even though her answer raised more questions than it answered, such as what exactly did she need to escape from?

"I actually thought about looking you up, but I wasn't sure if I should," she said.

He arched a brow. "Why not?"

Avery took a deep breath, and for a long, loaded moment, the space between them felt swollen with meaning. But then she just bit her lip and shrugged.

"Are those for me?" She smiled at the bouquet in his hand.

A wave of pleasure surged through him. Whatever her reason for being here, it was great to see her again. "They sure are."

"How very gentlemanly of you. Thank you." She took the flowers and held them close to her chest. Her soft brown eyes seemed lovelier than ever, mirroring the rich, dark centers of the sunflowers. "Do you want to come in while I put these in some water?"

She gestured toward the interior of the boarding house, which was the last place Finn wanted to be while Melba was around.

"Actually, since you seem so interested in the area, why don't I show you around town for a bit? I can even give you a tour of the ranch if you like."

"A tour of the ranch," she echoed. The flowers in her grip trembled. "*Your* ranch?"

Finn paused, remembering what she'd told him in Oklahoma about the supposed feud between their families. Once upon a time, Oscar Ellington and Maximilian Crawford had been friends. Best friends, according to Avery's father. They'd roomed together in college, both majoring in agriculture and ranch management. After graduation, they'd planned to go into business together, but at the last minute, Finn's father had changed his mind. He pulled out of the deal, and the friendship came to its tumultuous end.

"Sure," Finn said. He and Avery weren't their parents. He saw no reason why he couldn't take her to the Ambling A and walk the land with her, show her how the fall colors made the mountainside look as if it were aflame.

Although, if Oscar and Maximilian had turned their youthful dreams into a reality, the ranch wouldn't be his. It would be theirs—his and Avery's both.

Imagine that, he thought. *Being tied to Avery Ellington for life.*

He could think of worse fates.

But that would never happen. Ever. He wasn't even sure why he was entertaining the notion, other than the fact that his dad and Viv Dalton were dead set on putting an end to his independence.

"All right, then," Avery said, but her smile turned bittersweet. "Let's go."

Copper and gold leaves crunched beneath Avery's feet as she and Finn walked from his truck to the grand log cabin overlooking acres and acres of ranch land and glittering sunlit pastures where horses flicked their tails and grazed on shimmering emerald grass.

Calling it a cabin was a bit of a stretch. It looked more like a mansion made of Lincoln Logs, surrounded by a sprawling patio fashioned from artistically arranged river stones. The Rocky Mountains loomed in the background, rugged and golden. Enemy territory was quite lovely, it seemed.

Finn slipped his hand onto the small of her back as he led her toward the main house, and she tried her best to relax. An impossible task, considering that her father would probably disown her if he had any idea where she was right now. Finding out about the baby was going to kill him.

But she couldn't worry about that now. First, she had to figure out how to tell Finn, and that seemed more difficult than ever now that this little outing was beginning to feel like a date.

Does he have to be so charming?

It was the flowers—they'd completely thrown her off her game. Which was pathetic, considering how active Finn's Montana social life had become. He probably got a bulk discount at the nearest florist.

"This place is gorgeous," she said. "Do all your brothers live out here?"

Finn nodded. "Logan, Knox and Hunter have cottages on the property. Xander and his family just moved into their own ranch house in town. Wilder and I live in the main house with my dad."

His dad.

So Maximilian Crawford was *here* somewhere. Great.

"You look a million miles away all of a sudden." Finn paused on the threshold to study her. "Everything okay?"

No, nothing was okay. She felt huge and overly emotional, and he was still the same ridiculously handsome man, perfectly dashing in all his clueless daddy-to-be glory.

"Actually…" Her mouth went dry. She couldn't swallow, much less form the words she so desperately needed to say.

Tell him. Do it now.

"Yes?" He tilted his head, dark eyes glittering beneath the rim of his black Stetson.

Meeting his gaze felt impossible all of a sudden, so she glanced at his plain black T-shirt instead. But the way it hugged the solid wall of his chest was distracting to say the least.

"I, um…" She let out a lungful of air.

"You're beautiful, that's what you are. A sight for sore eyes. Do you have any idea how glad I am to see you?" Finn reached up and ran his hand along her jaw, caressing her cheek with the pad of his thumb.

It took every ounce of Avery's will-power not to lean into his touch and purr like a kitten. Her body was more than ready to just go with the flow, but her thoughts were screaming.

Tell him, you coward!

"I'm relieved to hear you say that." Butterflies took flight deep in Avery's belly—or maybe it was their baby doing backflips at the sound of its daddy's voice. She swallowed hard. "Because..."

Then all of a sudden, the front door swung open and she was rendered utterly speechless by the sight of her father's mortal enemy standing on the threshold with an enormous orange pumpkin tucked under one arm.

She recognized him in an instant. His picture appeared every year in the Crawford Meats annual report, and he looked exactly the same as his slick corporate portrait. Same deep tan and lined face, same devil-may-care expression.

Maximilian Crawford stared at her for a surprised beat. Then he glanced back and forth between her and Finn until his eyes narrowed into slits. "Well, well. Howdy, you two."

"Dad," Finn said. There was a hint of a warning in his voice, but Maximilian seemed to ignore it.

"Aren't you going to tell me what you're doing keeping company with Avery Ellington?" The older man smiled, but it didn't quite reach his eyes.

Maximilian Crawford had just smiled at her. She was surprised lightning didn't strike her on the spot. If her father were dead, he'd be spinning in his grave.

"Avery's just here for a friendly visit." Finn's hand moved to the small of her back again, and a shiver snaked its way up her spine. "I'm not sure you two have officially met. Avery, meet my dad, Maximilian."

"Hello, sir." She offered her hand.

He gave it a shake, but instead of letting go, he kept her hand clasped in his. "You're Oscar's little girl."

He was going there. *Okaaaay.*

"One and the same," she said, reminding herself that this man wasn't just her father's nemesis. He was also the grandfather of her unborn child.

"Right." He gave her hand a light squeeze and then finally released it. "I'm not sure if your daddy ever mentioned me, but he and I go way back."

Avery nodded. "I'm aware."

She shot a quick glance at Finn. The night they'd slept together in Oklahoma, he didn't seem to care much about any animosity between their families, but she'd wondered if he'd simply been downplaying things in order to avoid any awkwardness between them.

Not that she'd cared. She'd been more than ready to forget about anything that got in the way of their ongoing flirtation. Besides, they'd been miles away from Dallas. Just like the famous saying—what happens in Oklahoma stays in Oklahoma.

Unless it results in an accidental pregnancy.

"Interesting man, your father." Maximilian's expression turned vaguely nostalgic. "We were roommates back in the day. Almost went into business together. Truth be told, I occasionally miss those times."

Finn sneaked Avery a reassuring grin as his father's attitude softened somewhat.

"How's he doing? And your mom?" Maximilian shifted his pumpkin from one arm to the other. "Good, I hope."

Avery nodded. "They're great."

For now, anyway. Once she started showing, all bets were off.

"Avery's in town for a few days, so I thought I'd show her around a little bit." Finn eyed the pumpkin. "Tell me you're not on the way out here to try to carve that thing into a jack-o'-lantern."

"It's October. Of course that's what I'm going to do."

"Dad, this isn't Dallas. Halloween isn't for a few weeks. If you leave a carved pumpkin outside, it's going to get eaten up long before the thirty-first. The coyotes will probably get it before sunup." Finn shrugged. "If the elk don't get to it first."

"Fine. I'll take it inside after it's done. I've got five more to carve after this one. We can line them up by the fireplace. I just thought the place could use some holiday flair." Maximilian grinned. "Especially since we're welcoming a new little one to the family."

Avery coughed, and both men turned to look at her. "Excuse me. Little one?"

They couldn't possibly know. Could they?

"My brother Logan is a new stepdad.

He and his wife have a nine-month-old little girl, and my father suddenly wants us to believe he's transformed from a cattle baron into a doting grandfather." Finn narrowed his gaze at his dad.

"Oh." This seemed promising. It almost made her wish she planned on raising the baby closer to Montana, but that would be insane. She had a job back in Dallas. A family. A life. "How sweet."

Finn held out his hands to his father. "Why don't you leave the pumpkin carving to us? Manual labor of any kind isn't exactly your strong suit."

Maximilian glanced at Avery and lifted a brow. "You're willing to stick around long enough to help Finn with my mini pumpkin patch?"

Avery couldn't help but smile. She wasn't naive enough to believe Maximilian was just a harmless grandpa. He was a far more complicated man than that. On more than one occasion, she'd heard Finn refer to him as manipulative.

Even so, she had a difficult time reconciling the man standing in front of her—the one who wanted to carve half a dozen jack-o'-lanterns for his new baby granddaughter's first Halloween—with the backstabbing monster her father had been describing to her for as long as she could remember.

"I think that can be arranged," she said.

She still planned to tell Finn about the baby today. Of course she did. But what different could a few more hours make?

"I like her," Maximilian said as he handed the pumpkin over to Finn and slapped him hard on the back. "She seems like a keeper, son."

What on earth was she doing here?

A keeper.

Nope. No way, no how. She could have a dozen babies with Finn, but she'd never,

ever be a Crawford—not if her daddy had anything to do with it.

Avery set down her paring knife and wiped her hands on a dish towel so she could inspect the pumpkin she'd been attempting to carve. Its triangle-shaped eyes were uneven, and its wide, toothy grin was definitely lopsided. Overall, though, it was a decent effort.

Or at least she though it was until she took a closer look at what Finn had managed to produce in the same amount of time.

"Wait a minute." She frowned at twin jack-o'-lanterns on the table in front of him. "When did you start on the second one?"

He glanced at her pumpkin and stifled a grin. "Somewhere around the time you decided to give yours a square nose."

She swatted at him with the dish towel. The nose had started out as a triangle—

she wasn't quite sure how it had ended up as a square.

Finn laughed, ducking out of the way. He managed to catch the towel and snatch it away from her before it made contact with his head. His grin was triumphant, but it softened as he met her gaze.

"You've got a little something." He gestured toward the side of his face. "Right there."

Shocker. Avery wouldn't have been surprised to discover she was covered head to toe in pumpkin guts. The jack-o'-lantern struggle had been very real.

She wiped her cheek, and Finn shook his head, laughter dancing in his eyes.

"I just made it worse, didn't I?" she said, looking down at her orange hands.

"Afraid so. Here, let me." He cupped her face with irritatingly clean fingertips and dabbed at her cheek with the towel.

It was a perfectly innocent gesture.

Sweet, really. But Avery's heart felt like it was going to pound right out of her chest, and she had the completely inappropriate urge to kiss him as his gaze collided with hers.

She cleared her throat and backed away. She blamed pregnancy hormones…and the insanely gorgeous surroundings. Finn had set up their pumpkin-carving station on one of the log mansion's covered porches. It had a lovely, unobstructed view of the mountains, plus an enormous outdoor fireplace crafted from stone with a weathered wooden mantel. Any woman would have melted under the circumstances.

Avery kept having to remind herself that half the female population of Rust Creek Falls likely already had.

"You're shockingly good at this." She arched a brow at his two perfectly carved pumpkins in an effort to get her thoughts—and sensitive libido—back under control. "Do you have a degree in festive fall decorating I don't know about?"

"No, but I suppose it's fair to say there are indeed things you don't know about me. After all, our interactions have been pretty limited to business gatherings." Avery waited for Finn to crack a joke about their night together being the exception, but he didn't.

She wasn't altogether sure why that made her happy, but it did. "True."

He seemed different here than he'd been back in Dallas, and it was more than just a switch from tailored business suits to worn jeans and cowboy boots.

"So you like it here in Montana?" she asked.

"I do." Finn nodded and stared thoughtfully at the horizon, where a mist had gathered at the base of the mountain, creating a swirl of smoky autumn colors. "Life is different here. Richer, somehow. I always liked spending time on our ranch back in Texas, but somehow I never got out there much. I spent more time in boardrooms than I did with the herd. Does that make sense?"

Her face grew warm as he glanced at her. "It does."

Avery couldn't remember the last time she'd been to her own family ranch, much less spent any time with the herd. She'd spent more hours with Excel spreadsheets than she ever had with actual cattle.

Finn's gaze narrowed, and as if he could see straight inside her head, he said, "When was the last time you handfed a cow?"

Laughter bubbled up her throat. "Seriously? Never."

"Never?" He clutched his chest. "You're killing me, Princess."

Princess.

She usually hated it when he called her

that, but she decided to ignore Finn's pet name for her for the time being, mainly because it sort of fit, as much as she was loath to admit it.

He stood and offered her his hand. "Come on."

She placed her hand in his as if it were the most natural thing in the world, and he hauled her to her feet. "Where are we going?"

"You'll see." He winked, and it seemed to float right through her on butterfly wings. "You trust me, don't you, Princess?"

That was a loaded question if she'd ever heard one. "Should I?"

He gave her hand a squeeze in lieu of an actual answer, then shot her a lazy grin and tugged her in the direction of the barn.

Right. That's what I thought.

Of course she couldn't trust him. He might seem at home here on the farm in a way that made her think there was more to Finn Crawford than met the eye, but just because a man could carve a jack-o'-lantern and went all soft around the edges when he talked about animals didn't mean he was ready for a family.

Avery slipped her hand from his and crossed her arms. "What about the pumpkins? Won't coyotes come and devour them if we leave?"

Her mind had snagged on Finn's casual reference to coyotes earlier, probably because the biggest threat to jack-o'-lanterns in her Dallas neighborhood were mischievous teens.

He glanced over her shoulder toward the porch, where Maximilian had begun cleaning up their mess and hauling the pumpkins inside.

Avery rolled her eyes. "And you call *me* a princess."

He flashed a grin. "Touché."

He took hold of her hand again, and

she let him, because his rakish smile and down-home charm were getting to her. And honestly, considering she was pregnant with the man's baby, it was a little late to be worried about hand-holding.

The barn was cool and sweet-smelling, like hay and sunshine. It reminded Avery of the horseback riding lessons she'd had as a little girl. She'd ridden English, of course. No rodeos or trail rides for the daughter of Oscar Ellington. Her childhood and teen years had been about posh country club horse shows and debutante balls.

Her thoughts snagged briefly on what might be in store for her unborn child. If she raised the baby by herself, in Dallas, she'd be setting her son or daughter up for the same type of upbringing she'd had. Her father would see to it.

But was that really what Avery wanted?

She wasn't so sure, and suddenly she couldn't seem to focus on the many difficult decisions she needed to address. She couldn't seem to focus on *anything* except Finn's cocky, lopsided grin and the cozy hayloft in the barn's shady rafters. Wouldn't it be nice to be kissed in a place like that?

For the last time, calm down, pregnancy hormones!

"It's really lovely here," she said, glancing around the sun-dappled space. Horses poked their heads over the tops of stable doors and whinnied as they walked past.

"It's nice. We've got a lot more space than we had in Texas."

"So your move here is permanent, then." She held her breath. What was she saying?

Of course it was permanent. This was Finn's new home.

"Oh, yeah." He nodded and guided her toward the corner of the barn, where a few barrels were lined up along the wall.

Avery wondered how much of his enthusiasm for Rust Creek Falls had to do with his overactive dating life…and just how many women he'd brought out to the Ambling A for this quaint little tour. On second thought, maybe she was better off without that information.

"Here we go." Finn reached into one of the barrels and pulled out a few ears of colorful calico corn—sapphire blues, deep burgundies and ruby reds. It almost looked like he was holding a handful of gemstones.

He offered her a few ears, and she took them. "Pretty. Are we adding a little harvest decor to the jack-o'-lantern display for your niece?"

"No, my dad donated a big batch of harvest corn to the town for the autumn festival, and we've got a few barrels left over. So now what you've got there is a treat for the cattle."

She glanced down at the corn and back up at Finn. He'd been dead serious about spending hands-on time with the herd. "You mean cow treats are a thing?"

"Everyone deserves a little something special now and then, don't you think?" His eyes gleamed.

Avery was a firm believer in this sentiment. It was precisely how she ended up with her most recent Louis Vuitton handbag. It's also how she'd ended up in bed with Finn Crawford on her last business trip.

She blinked up at him and prayed he couldn't read her mind. "Absolutely."

Finn couldn't shake the feeling that there was something different about Avery. When he couldn't figure out exactly what it was, he realized the difference wasn't just one thing. *Everything* about her seemed different somehow.

Then again, he'd never seen her this way before. Finn knew the proper, corporate Avery—Princess Avery, as he liked to call her, much to her irritation. He'd never seen the coppery highlights that fresh sunshine brought out in her tumbling waves of hair. He'd certainly never wrapped his arms around her from behind and held her close in a pasture while she tried to feed an overeager cow an ear of calico corn.

Every time the Hereford's big head got close to her hand, she pulled it back and squealed. The poor confused cow glanced back and forth between Avery and Finn and then stared longingly at the ear of corn.

"Cows seems significantly bigger up close," Avery said.

"This one's harmless, I promise. She's a gentle giant, wouldn't hurt a fly." He took hold of Avery's hand and guided the corn toward the cow's mouth.

The Hereford snorted in gratitude and wrapped her wide tongue around the corncob.

"Ahh! I'm doing it." Avery laughed, and the cow's ears swiveled to and fro.

The corn was gone within a matter of minutes, and Avery beamed at Finn over her shoulder. "Can I give her another one?"

"Sure." He handed her another ear of the colorful corn.

Avery fed it to the cow all on her own this time, giggling in delight when the animal made happy slurping sounds.

"This is the most hands-on I've ever gotten with cattle." She turned in his arms so she was facing him and shot him a conciliatory look. "You were right. It gives me a whole new appreciation for what we do."

Finn had been a rancher all his life, and he'd never seen anyone take such sheer delight in feeding cattle before. It was a shame Avery's father had never taken the time to teach her the ins and outs of hands-on ranch management in addition to crunching numbers and networking. But he wasn't about to bring up Oscar Ellington and spoil the mood. The man hated him, apparently, although Finn probably never would have known as much if Avery hadn't mentioned it over martinis in the darkened bar in Oklahoma.

"Then it's a good thing I dragged you away from the boarding house," he said.

Avery's hands found their way to his chest, and their eyes met for a beat until she seemed to realize she was touching him.

"Right, but I should probably be getting back." She took a backward step and collided with the cow.

She let out a loud moo, and Avery jumped back into his arms.

He couldn't help but laugh. "Relax, Princess. Everything's fine."

"It's really not." She shook her head, but at the same time melted into him.

And this time, when her hands landed on his pecs, they stayed.

Finn could feel her heart beating hard against his chest, and her eyes grew dark...dreamy...as her lips parted ever so slightly.

He'd never wanted to kiss a woman more in his life, but he was still a little thrown by her words.

It's really not.

He had no clue what she meant. Everything certainly seemed fine. She felt so good in his arms. So soft. So warm. And he especially liked the way she was suddenly focusing intently on his mouth.

But he wasn't about to kiss her if it wasn't what she wanted. He inhaled a ragged breath and cast her a questioning glance.

"Honestly, I should go." She lifted her arms and wound them around his neck.

"Avery." He half groaned her name.

If he couldn't kiss her, he was going to

have to take her arms and unwind them himself. He wasn't going to last another minute with her pressed against him, looking up at him like she wanted to devour him. He was only human.

But just as his fingers slipped around her wrists, she rose up on her tiptoes and kissed him so hard that she nearly knocked him over. Her mouth was warm and ready, and before he fully grasped what was happening, her fingertips slid into his hair, knocking his Stetson to the ground.

Finn didn't give a damn about the hat. He didn't give a damn about much of anything except the woman in his arms and the way she was murmuring his name against his lips, as if they were suddenly right back in the middle of that surreal, sublime night in Oklahoma.

He'd been thinking about that night for four long months, convinced their paths would never cross again. And now here she was, as beautiful and maddening as ever.

He nipped softly at her bottom lip and she let out a breathy sigh, and somewhere in the back of his mind, he wondered again what exactly she was doing in Montana, so far off the beaten path. He wasn't altogether sure he bought her business trip explanation. No one had business this far out. He didn't dare ask, lest he ruin the moment.

But he didn't have to, because the moment came to an abrupt end, thanks to an earsplitting chorus of hungry moos.

Their eyes flew open, and Avery blinked, horrified. Whether she was more shaken by the sight of half a dozen cows suddenly surrounding them in the pasture or the fact that she'd thrown herself at him, he wasn't entirely sure. He hoped it was the former, but he wouldn't bet his life on it.

"I, um…" She bit her lip. "I'm sorry about that."

"Avery, talk to me. Tell me what's wrong."

One of the cows nudged her, and she shook her head. "Nothing. Nothing's wrong. I'm just… I'm sorry. I should really…"

"It's okay." He nodded, still thoroughly baffled but getting nowhere amid a sea of cattle and half-eaten harvest corn. "I'll take you home."

The look of relief on her face was almost enough to make him think he'd imagined the fact that she'd just kissed him silly. Not quite, though.

Not quite.

Chapter Four

"Tell me again why we're doing this?" Melba's gaze cut toward Avery as she slid one foot to rest alongside her opposite ankle in a wobbly modified version of tree pose. The baby goat bleated in her arms.

Avery had to give Melba credit. She was really being a good sport about the whole goat yoga thing.

"People pay good money to do this in the city. I promise," Avery said as she settled into her own tree pose.

Thanks in part to yoga with animals being all the rage on Instagram, her yoga studio in Dallas had held a special goat yoga fund-raiser after the most recent Texas hurricane and ended up raising thousands for storm relief. How a private fitness boutique in the luxury Highland Park neighborhood procured a dozen tiny goats for the day was a mystery Avery couldn't begin to fathom. But her life in Rust Creek Falls seemed to be teeming with farm animals.

Avery placed her hands in prayer position and closed her eyes. "Think of it as pet therapy and yoga all rolled into one. It's supposed to clear the mind and release loads of feel-good endorphins."

Plus Avery just needed the company. Since her visit to the Ambling A with Finn two days ago, she'd practically been a hermit. She'd shut herself up in her room, poking her head out only for meals and a few speed-yoga sessions, lest Finn turn up at the front door again.

She wasn't ready to see him—not after that kiss. Making out with the father of her baby before he even knew she was pregnant was definitely *not* part of the plan. Nor was making out with him afterward. Her mission was pretty straightforward: face her moral responsibility to tell Finn about the baby, then hightail it back to Dallas and get on with her life as a single-mom-to-be.

The plan involved zero kissing whatsoever.

The trouble was, when Finn dropped her off at the boarding house after she threw herself at him in the pasture, he'd asked if he could see her again and she'd said yes. How could she not? They still needed to have a very important conversation. But she needed some time to get her bearings first, and she definitely didn't need to go back to the Ambling

A. It was far too cozy over there, with all the pumpkin carving and the cows munching on harvest corn. What would happen next time? A moonlit hayride?

No.

Because there wouldn't be a next time. She should have never set foot on Crawford property in the first place. Telling him about the pregnancy needed to take place on neutral territory. Someplace safe.

"Is your mind clear yet?" Avery cracked her eyes open to check on Melba.

The older woman gave her a blank look. The baby goat in her arms let out a warbly bleat, and Melba bit back a smile. "Afraid not, dear."

That made two of them.

"Melba!" someone called from inside the house, and before either of them could respond, the door flew open and Old Gene strode onto the porch.

He took in the yoga mats, then glanced

back and forth between their tree poses. "What in the world is going on out here?"

"What does it look like?" Melba sniffed. "Avery is teaching me some of her fancy yoga moves."

"You're doing yoga?" He gaped at her as if she'd just sprouted another head. "With the goat?"

"Avery says it's a thing." Melba glanced at her for confirmation.

"Indeed it is." Avery nodded. "Very on trend."

"I'm old, but I'm not dead. I can still learn new things. Besides, you've been gone all morning. Someone had to watch the wee thing." Melba scratched the baby goat behind the ears. When she appeared to realize what she was doing, she stopped.

Her resistance was crumbling where the goat was concerned, much to Avery's amusement. Not that she was surprised. Melba was a natural caretaker. It was what made the boarding house such a nice place to stay.

Avery, however, was still avoiding any and all hands-on interaction with the tiny creature. She knew next to nothing the about farm animals, her recent cattle experience notwithstanding. The one thing she did know, though, was that it should probably have a name by now.

"Have you thought of what you want to call the poor goat yet?" she asked Old Gene.

His gaze darted to his wife. "I thought Melba might want to do the honors."

"Oh, no, you don't." She dumped the baby goat in Gene's arms, where it landed in a heap of tiny hooves, soft bleats and furry orange coat. "If I name her, that means we're keeping her. Nice try, but no."

Melba gave her eyes a mighty roll and huffed off in the direction of the kitchen.

Okay, then. Namaste.

Avery smiled to herself as she bent down to roll up the yoga mats. "Give it a few more days, Gene. I think the little kid is growing on her. Where were you off to this morning?"

Old Gene had been notably absent at breakfast. For once, Claire's homemade cinnamon rolls had lasted past 9:00 a.m. Avery had indulged in seconds, since she was eating for two.

"I was at a planning meeting for the upcoming autumn festival over at the high school, but then the delivery of hay for the hay maze arrived and needed unloading. The last time I tossed a hay bale around, I threw my back out. So I left that to the younger folks and scooted on home." He set the goat on the ground, and the animal teetered toward the grass beyond Avery's makeshift yoga area on the porch.

"That sounds like a wise choice," Avery said. The thought of Melba taking care of an incapacitated Old Gene on top of the boarding house and an orphaned goat was too unnerving to contemplate. "So is this autumn festival a big thing around here?"

Finn had mentioned the festival, and her curiosity was definitely piqued.

Old Gene nodded and crossed his arms as he watched the baby goat bounce around the yard. "Yes, ma'am. It certainly is."

"What's it like?"

"Let's see. The festival starts off with two weeks of fall-themed activities in the evenings and then ends with a Halloween party in the school gym. It's a big family event. The kids dress up in costumes, there are always a lot of Halloween-themed games and Melba brings her famous caramel apples. You'd love it."

Avery grinned.

She'd never been to a small-town festival before. And the last Halloween party she'd attended had been a stuffy masquerade ball at the country club. Adults only. The costumes had all been extravagant rentals and the guests dined on delicate hors d'oeuvres and cocktails. A quaint small-town Halloween did indeed sound lovely.

Old Gene dragged his gaze away from the goat and studied her for a moment. "You'll still be here in two weeks, right?"

"Oh." She straightened and hugged her yoga mat to her chest. "I'm not sure. It kind of depends..."

On how much longer I put off the inevitable.

"I doubt it," she added.

She'd already been away from the office far too long. Her parents thought she was off on a spa getaway with friends. That excuse would wear thin eventually—sooner rather than later.

Old Gene refocused his attention on the goat, and Avery noticed his shoulders sag a little bit. "That's too bad. Melba is going to worry about you when you're gone. She has a soft spot for you, you know."

Guilt nagged at Avery's conscience. She'd known for weeks that Melba suspected she was on the run from a bad relationship, and she'd done nothing to alleviate such worries. Letting her believe in some fictional ex-boyfriend seemed so much easier than trying to explain the truth.

"I know." An ache knotted in her throat.

She liked it here. She liked Melba and Old Gene. She even sort of liked the goat. She would have, anyway, if its very presence didn't remind her of her complete and total lack of maternal instincts. The real reason she'd yet to try to bottle-feed it was because she was afraid she'd mess everything up and the goat would reject her.

How sad was that?

"My wife wouldn't try yoga for just anyone, especially not with this trouble-maker." Old Gene scooped the goat into his arms and stuck a foot out in front of him as if he were trying to kick an imaginary soccer ball. "What about me? Am I doing it right?"

Avery snorted with laughter. "You're nailing it, Gene."

"Who says you can't teach an old dog new tricks?" He flashed a triumphant smile and carried the goat inside.

Its little head rested on Old Gene's shoulder, and the animal fluttered its long eyelashes at Avery as they disappeared from view.

She wondered if the sentiment applied to herself, as well. She wasn't exactly old, but aside from the fact that she wasn't in a relationship with her baby's father, she was woefully unprepared for motherhood. She'd never once changed a diaper. As an only child, she'd never spent much time around children, either. She hadn't even babysat for extra money as a teenager. She hadn't needed to. Her parents had always been more than happy to give her everything she wanted, including a job.

There was more truth to Finn's nickname for her than she wanted to admit.

Princess.

She took a shaky inhale of crisp autumn air and tried to ignore the nagging feeling that her charmed existence was about to come to an abrupt end. Maximilian Crawford might have fond memories of her father, but the feeling definitely wasn't mutual. Oscar Ellington was going to hit the roof when he found out she'd slept with Finn.

Ready or not, life as Avery knew it was about to change.

Finn leaned against the vast kitchen counter in the main house of the Ambling A while he stared at the screen of his iPhone and frowned. Four missed calls showed on his display, and not one of them was Avery.

He sighed, put the phone down and then picked it back up again just in case.

Still nothing. Damn it.

He did his best to ignore the fact that he was acting like a lovesick teenager and jabbed at the power button of the high-end espresso machine his father had imported from Europe. You could take Maximilian Crawford out of the big city, but you couldn't take the big city out of Maximilian.

"There you are," the older man said as he strolled into view.

Speak of the devil. "Hello, Dad."

Finn flipped a switch, and dark, aromatic liquid began to fill his cup. Black, like his mood.

"Where have you been, son?" Maximilian jammed his hands on his hips.

"Viv Dalton has been trying to get ahold of you all day."

Finn was well aware of the fact that the matchmaker/wedding planner had been trying to reach him. She'd been blowing his phone up all morning, hence the missed call notifications.

"I had meetings all day in Billings. I have a job, remember?" He sipped his coffee, then arched a brow at his father. "And contrary to whatever you've started to believe, it doesn't involve carrying on the family name."

That's what his five brothers were for.

Maximilian glared at Finn's phone, sitting quietly on the marble countertop. "You need to call her back. She's set up a date for you this evening."

Just as Finn suspected. Ordinarily, this bit of news would have taken the edge off his stormy mood. Now, not so much.

"No." Finn shook his head.

"What do you mean, no?" Maximilian looked at him as if he'd just sprouted two heads.

Finn didn't really blame him. He'd nearly surprised himself, as well. "I mean, no. I can't."

Can't was a stretch. *Won't* was more like it. After recently spending the day with Avery, he just didn't have it in him for another date with another total stranger. Frankly, the idea didn't sound appealing at all.

What the heck had gotten into him?

Avery's spur-of-the-moment kiss, that's what.

Finn cleared his throat and took another scalding gulp of coffee.

"Balderdash." Maximilian waved a dismissive hand. "Viv has been going the extra mile to line up these dates for you. Unless you have other plans, you'll go."

Much to his dismay, Finn had zero plans. Avery had agreed to see him again, but he'd been trying to give her some space, since she'd seemed so rattled by the kiss. He thought it best to let her contact him instead of the other way around.

He just hadn't bargained on it taking so long...or that waiting for her call would make him feel like an insecure kid hoping for an invitation to prom.

"I do have other plans, actually." He set down his coffee cup with a little too much force, picked up his phone and tucked it into his pocket as he strode toward the door.

"Since when?" a disbelieving Maximilian said to his back.

Since now.

"Finn." Avery wrapped her arms around her middle and glanced back and forth between the father of her baby and Old Gene, sitting across from one another at the big farm table in the kitchen of the boarding house. "I didn't realize you were here."

"I gave Melba a shout upstairs and asked her to send you down." Old Gene shrugged.

The baby goat was snuggled in his lap with its spindly legs tucked beneath itself. What must Finn think? He lived on that massive log cabin estate out at the Ambling A, and their kitchen looked like a scene out of *Green Acres*.

She blinked.

Their kitchen?

You don't actually live *here, remember. This is temporary.*

"Yes, you did holler for me to send Avery to the kitchen." Melba bustled into the room behind Avery and paused, hands on her sturdy hips. "But you didn't mention we had company."

Finn pushed back from the table and stood. "Hello, Mrs. Strickland." He set amused eyes on Avery. "Hi."

"Hi." Her face went warm, suddenly bashful to be interacting with Finn in front of the Stricklands, which was patently ridiculous. They weren't kids, after all.

But Melba and Old Gene were nurturing in a way that Avery's parents had never been. Not only was it making her think long and hard about what sort of mother she hoped to be, but it was also making her fall more in love with Rust Creek Falls every day.

Of course the fact that there was currently a handsome cowboy smiling at her didn't hurt, either.

"What brings you by, Mr. Crawford?" Melba, apparently the only woman in Montana impervious to Finn's charms, crossed her arms.

"I thought Avery might like to take a ride out to the maple syrup farm." He winked at Avery—just a quick, nearly imperceptible flutter of his lashes, but all the air in the room seemed to gather in her lungs. She was breathless all of a sudden. "If that's okay with you folks, of course."

Avery bit back a smile. He was asking Melba and Old Gene for permission to take her on a date, which was kind of adorable. Too adorable to resist, actually.

"Well, I don't know," Melba said.

"Don't be silly, dear." Old Gene stood. "It's fine. Avery would probably love it out there. It's so colorful this time of year."

The goat bleated its agreement. Melba, outnumbered, sighed.

"I'll go get changed." Avery pulled her T-shirt down in an effort to more fully cover her midsection. She was still wearing yoga pants, and chances were they showed off an entirely different body than the one Finn had seen naked a few months ago.

"It's a farm." Finn tilted his head and

looked Avery up and down. "You're not planning on slipping into one of your pencil skirts, are you?"

She laughed a little too loud. Her days of fitting into a pencil skirt were over. For five months, minimum. "No, just something cozy."

Translation: something baggy enough to hide her rapidly expanding baby bump.

She slipped into one of her new flannel purchases, a soft pair of leggings and bouncy sneakers. Melba seemed a little less hostile when she returned to the kitchen. Finn must have really turned on the charm, because when they left for the maple syrup farm, Melba sent them off with a thermos of her special apple cider.

"The Stricklands really seem to enjoy having you around," Finn said as they passed the Welcome to Rust Creek Falls sign on the outskirts of town.

The smells of cinnamon and spice swirled in the cab of Finn's truck, wrapping around them like a plush blanket. Avery closed her eyes and took a deep inhale. "Mmm. Melba and Old Gene are the best, aren't they?"

"They are, but I'm not sure the feeling is mutual, especially where Melba is concerned."

"She's just a little protective, that's all." Avery nearly gasped at how colorful the trees looked as they moved deeper and deeper into the countryside and farther away from Rust Creek Falls.

Finn shot her a mischievous glance. "Do you think you need protecting from me, Princess?"

Avery thought about the warning Melba had given her about Finn after they'd bumped into him at the general store.

Finn isn't right for a nice girl like you.
She arched a brow. "You tell me. Do I?"

Finn responded with a wide grin that told her he definitely hadn't forgotten about the way she thrown herself at him in the pasture at the Ambling A. Maybe Melba had it wrong and he was the one who needed protecting.

Avery straightened in her seat. Finn could smile all he wanted. She intended to take this time together to have a serious discussion with him. There would be no more kissing. Not today, anyway.

Except there was.

Once again, Avery fell completely under the spell of Finn in his natural habitat. Why did he suddenly seem like he belonged on the pages of a hot cowboys calendar rather than in the boardrooms where she usually ran into him back in Texas?

The maple syrup farm was much quieter than she anticipated. She'd expected trees with sap buckets attached and the hum of boilers in the nearby sugarhouse. But as Finn explained, the sapping season usually ran from February until mid-April or so. The farms still had a good number of visitors during autumn, though, due to the spectacular fall colors of the sugar maple trees.

Avery could hardly believe her eyes. After they'd stopped by the farm's quaint little gift shop and Avery purchased glass bottles of syrup in varying colors of amber, they went for a walk in the sugar bush. The deeper into the woods they wandered, the closer together the trees grew, until she and Finn were surrounded by nothing but blazing red. Crimson leaves floated through the air like radiant snowflakes, and when they came upon a tiny white chapel nestled far into the cluster of maples, Avery was completely and utterly enchanted.

That was her only explanation for what happened next. It was as if the beautiful surroundings had indeed made her fall under a magical spell, because when she looked at Finn in the dappled sunlight of the fiery woods, her canvas bag of maple syrup slipped from her hand and fell to the ground with a soft thud. She wrapped her arms around the father of her baby and kissed him, long and deep. She kissed him so hard that the force of it seemed to shake loose the leaves from the surrounding sugar maples, until at last she had to pull away to catch her breath.

What was happening to her? Why did she keep losing her head like this?

"I'm so sorry," she said, backing away against the solid trunk of a maple tree. Good. Maybe it would knock some sense into her. "I don't know why I keep doing that."

Finn gave her a tender smile that slowly built into a full-wattage grin. Avery's cheeks burned with heat, and she suspected her face had gone as red as the surrounding foliage.

But like the gentleman that he was, her

Texas-businessman-turned-Montana-cowboy spared her the embarrassment of saying anything. He simply bent to pick up her discarded bag, then took her by the hand and walked her back down the forest trail, leaving the kiss behind.

Just another of their secrets.

Chapter Five

Finn returned to the Ambling A after taking Avery back to the boarding house to find his dad and his brother Hunter fully immersed in a craft project with Hunter's six-year-old daughter, Wren.

The two men looked woefully out of place in their ranch attire while doing something with paper plates full of paint. Finn wasn't entirely sure what they were trying to accomplish, but Wren seemed as pleased as punch, which he supposed was the objective of the messy affair.

He took it all in with bemused interest and cocked an eyebrow at his father. "This is a surprise. For some reason, I thought you had plans tonight with one of your lady friends."

It was a logical assumption. On any given Friday night, Maximilian typically had a date. Sometimes two. When he wasn't preoccupied with meddling into his sons' love lives, of course.

"I do." Maximilian ruffled Wren's fair blond hair. "With this little lady right here."

Wren gigged and made jazz hands at Finn, her palms and fingers dripping orange paint onto the copies of the Rust Creek Falls *Gazette* that provided a protective covering for the table. "We're making handprint leaves, Uncle Finn. Do you want to make one, too?"

Large sheets of manila paper were scattered in front of her, decorated with yellow, orange and red handprints that had been fashioned into leaves with the help of stems and leafy veins drawn in brown magic marker.

"It looks like the three of you have got it covered." Finn eyed his brother. "Where on earth did you come up with this?"

Hunter shrugged. "Pinterest."

"Pinterest?" Finn bit back a smile. If anyone actually needed Viv Dalton's dating service, it was Hunter. Most definitely.

"What?" Hunter said, as if perusing Pinterest for kids' craft projects was something all of the Crawford brothers did on a daily basis.

"Nothing." Finn shook his head. It was actually really sweet how his brother had immersed himself into being both a father and mother to Wren. Not that he'd had much of a choice.

Still, it was pretty amusing seeing his rough-and-tumble brother and father sitting around doing arts and crafts on a Friday night. He was used to them doing things like roping calves and cutting hay, not finger-painting.

"I'm going up to bed. See you all in the morning." Finn faked a yawn and headed toward the stairs, eager to shut himself in his room before Maximilian had a chance to question him about his whereabouts.

"Hold up there, son."

Too late.

"Where have you been off to tonight?" Maximilian frowned down at the mess of paint in front of him. Clearly he'd skipped the Pinterest tutorial. "The young woman Viv wanted to introduce you to called here a little while ago and said she hadn't heard from you."

Finn's jaw clenched shut tight. *Give it a rest, old man. I'm handling my own love life just fine these days.*

And since when had Viv started giving out his phone number?

"I was with Avery Ellington," he said.

There. Maybe if he threw Maximilian a bone, his father would leave him alone for once.

"Is that right?" Maximilian's eyebrows furrowed and then released. "Glad to hear it. The Ellington apple seems to have fallen quite far from the tree. You two make a fine couple."

"Right." Hunter let out a snort as he drew another stem onto one of Wren's handprint leaves. "As if Finn is actually serious about her."

Hunter's casual dismissal of Finn's feelings about Avery rubbed him the wrong way, although he wasn't entirely sure why. She was only in town temporarily, and as Finn himself had reiterated time and again, he wasn't looking for anything serious.

"He's seen her more than once. For

your brother, that's serious," Maximilian said.

Hunter nodded. "Point taken."

Finn's chest grew tight. Why had he thought it was ever a good idea to live under the same roof as his family? "Are you two enjoying yourselves?"

"I am." Wren wiggled in her chair.

"Yes. You are, sweetheart. And I'm glad." Finn narrowed his gaze at his father. "But you need to calm down. Avery and I are just casually seeing each other until she goes back to Texas. It doesn't even qualify as a relationship."

Right... That's why you can't stop thinking about her.

He shifted his weight from one foot to the other, suddenly acutely uncomfortable with the direction this conversation was headed.

"Would it be so awful if she stayed in Montana?" Maximilian pressed his palm into a paper plate full of yellow paint.

Finn couldn't help wishing he'd accidentally spill it down the front of his snap-button Western shirt. "I'm surprised you're pressing the issue. Aren't you and her father are supposed to be mortal enemies?"

"Ellington or not, Avery seems good for you." Maximilian waved a hand, sending yellow paint splatters flying, much to Wren's amusement. "Her daddy and I haven't spoken in years. Maybe all that mess is simply water under the bridge."

Finn somehow doubted Avery's dad saw it that way.

"Regardless, I'm not in a relationship with his daughter." Finn's head hurt all of a sudden. He sighed. "We're just…"

Words failed him.

What *were* they doing? Hell if he knew. Nor did he have any idea why he was still standing around trying to explain it to his meddling father and smart-ass brother.

"You're just what, exactly?" The twinkle in Maximilian's eyes was as brilliant as a three-carat diamond engagement ring from Tiffany.

"Never mind. I'm going to bed." Finn ignored the suggestive smirks aimed his way and headed to his suite.

He didn't have the first clue what he and Avery were doing. One minute she was throwing herself at him, and the next she was knocking her head into a tree. It should have been making him crazy. And it was...

But in a good way—a way that had him counting the minutes until he could see her again. The warmth of Avery's sultry mouth had suddenly become the last thing he thought about before he drifted off to sleep and his first memory upon waking. Because whatever was really going on between them, Finn liked it.

He liked it a whole heck of a lot.

* * *

The third time Finn showed up unannounced at Strickland's, Avery was ready.

Call it intuition, or chalk it up to wishful thinking—Avery greatly preferred to think of it as the former. Either way, when he showed up bright and early the morning following their trip to the maple syrup farm, no one was surprised. Not her, not Melba, not Old Gene.

Not even the baby goat. The tiny animal woke from her nap on her dog bed by the back door and kicked her little hooves as Melba escorted Finn into the kitchen.

"Look who's here," she said, wiping her hands on her apron. "Again."

Melba seemed to be doing her best to keep up her general dislike of Finn, but the sparkle in her eye told Avery he was wearing her down. The tote bag full of maple syrup in his hands probably didn't hurt.

"Who wants pancakes?" Finn said, winking at Avery.

The baby goat bleated, and Avery couldn't help but smile.

Melba narrowed her gaze at Finn. "Pancakes aren't on the menu this morning."

Claire had whipped up her famous ham biscuits, which were up for grabs in the dining room. Avery had already eaten one, but she wouldn't turn down pancakes with real maple syrup. Not when she was eating for two.

"I thought I'd make them." Finn reached into his bag and extracted a box of organic pancake mix. "Pumpkin spice. Who's in?"

Had Finn Crawford just waltzed into Melba Strickland's home and announced he was going to cook? Oh, this was going to be good. Such a bold move was sure to either win her over or make her an enemy for life.

Old Gene's eyebrows shot clear to his hairline. Avery had to the bite the inside of her cheek to keep from laughing.

"What do you say, Mrs. Strickland?" Finn shot the older woman his most devastating bad-boy grin, and against all odds, it worked.

"Fine." She untied her apron and handed it to Finn. "If you insist. But you'll need to clean up after yourself. Claire and I won't abide a messy kitchen."

She paused a beat, then added, "And call me Melba."

"Yes, ma'am." Finn's grin widened as he tied the frilly apron around his waist.

He looked utterly ridiculous in his boots, jeans and Melba's lacy kitchen attire, but then again, Avery was still snug in her flannel pajamas.

"Come on, dear." Old Gene folded the newspaper he'd been reading into a neat square and pushed back from the kitchen table. "Let's leave these two young things alone for a spell."

Melba cast a questioning glance at Avery, and she nodded. "Go put your feet up. We'll let you know when the pancakes are ready."

The thought of Melba actually putting her feet up was almost laughable, but with a little added encouragement from Gene, she finally vacated the kitchen.

"I think she's starting to like you," Avery said after the swinging door closed behind the Stricklands.

"Good." Finn cocked his head. "Should I be worried about why she didn't like me to begin with?"

That would be due to your reputation as a serial womanizer.

Avery picked up the box of pancake mix and stared intently at the directions. She wasn't about to comment on Finn's overactive social life. Although, since she'd run into him at the general store, he hadn't had time to go on any dates. He seemed to be spending all of his free time with her.

Not that she was complaining. She'd definitely been enjoying his company. Truth be told, she enjoyed it far too much—hence the rather embarrassing habit she'd developed of kissing him whenever the mood struck her. Which was often.

But Avery had to give Finn credit. He still hadn't tried to get her into bed again, which she considered a major point in his favor. Instead of assuming they'd take up right where they'd left off in Oklahoma, he was wooing her.

And it was working. Melba wasn't the only one around the boarding house who'd developed a soft spot for Finn.

You're not supposed to be dating *him. It's a little late for that, isn't it?*

The box of pancake mix slipped through

Avery's fingers, and Finn caught it before it hit the floor.

"Whoa there, butterfingers," he said, but affection glowed in his eyes. He gave her a lopsided grin, and her heart pounded with such force that she wondered if he could hear it beneath the thick layer of her flannel pajama top.

If she wasn't careful, she was going to kiss him again, right there in the boarding house kitchen.

She grabbed the first thing she could get her hands on—Claire's favorite cast-iron skillet—and held it in front of her. A shield. "You need some help with those pancakes, cowboy?"

"Not really." He reached toward her and tucked a wayward lock of hair behind her ear. "But I'd never turn down a beautiful woman in pj's."

So I've heard.

She forced a smile. "All right, then. Let's do this."

* * *

Even though Finn's hands were occupied pouring batter and flipping pancakes, he was having serious trouble keeping them to himself.

Avery danced around him in her plaid pajamas, giving the batter an extra stir here and there, and there was something about her high, swinging ponytail and slippered feet he found adorably irresistible. He even found himself fantasizing that his mornings could start like this every day if he and Avery were a real couple.

If they were married, for example.

"Oops." Avery winced. "I think you're burning that one."

Finn blinked and refocused his attention on the cast-iron skillet in front of him, where smoke had begun rising from the lopsided circle of batter in its center. Oops indeed.

He scooped up the smoldering remains

with a spatula and dumped them in the trash. "We've still got a pretty good stack going."

"Good, because I think there's only enough batter for a few more." She handed him a semi-full measuring cup.

Finn took it, emptied it into the pan and handed it back to her, arching a brow when her fingertips brushed against his. Did she feel it, too? That little jolt of electricity that happened every time they touched?

The sudden flush of color in her peaches-and-cream complexion told him that indeed she did. "If you keep looking at me like that, cowboy, you're going to burn the next one, too."

He didn't much care. He wasn't even hungry, and there was already a towering stack of pumpkin-spiced goodness for Avery and the Stricklands.

The pancakes had been an excuse to see her again. That, and an attempt to get on Melba's good side, since she apparently had decided he wasn't good enough for Avery. When it came right down to it, he tended to agree. Avery was out of his league. She was the kind of woman who deserved to be wined and dined, whisked off to Paris for a romantic weekend getaway, swept off her feet with a surprise proposal.

Finn frowned down at the frying pan. For a man who had absolutely no interest in marriage, the antiquated institution certainly seemed to be occupying a large portion of his thoughts all of a sudden. He blamed his father. And Viv Dalton. And his brothers, three of whom had already fallen like dominoes. Being surrounded by so much marital bliss was messing with his head in a major way.

Things with Avery were exactly as he'd described them to Maximilian earlier. Casual. They were just enjoying each other's company until she went back to Texas.

Sure you are. Because playing house like this is just the sort of thing you usually do with women you're dating.

He flipped the last pancake on top of the stack and tried not to think about what the other Crawford men would say if they could see him now. Truthfully, he didn't much care what they thought. He was enjoying getting to know Avery better.

That didn't mean he wasn't counting down the minutes until she was back in his bed. He definitely was, and the minutes felt like they were getting longer and longer. But he and Avery were under the watchful gaze of Rust Creek Falls now, not on their own in the middle of Oklahoma. The Stricklands were old-fashioned folks, and as much as he wanted to, scooping Avery into his arms and carrying her upstairs to bed simply wasn't an option. Neither was asking her to spend the night at the Ambling A, for obvious reasons.

He wiped his hands on Melba's apron, and before he could stop himself, he said, "Will you go away with me next weekend?"

"Um. You want to go away together?" Avery's eyes went wide. Perhaps he should have removed the frilly apron before suggesting a romantic getaway. "Where?"

Anywhere, damn it.

"A nice B&B someplace. I can take a look around and find someplace special." He ditched the spatula, took a step closer and planted a hand on the counter on either side of her, hemming her in. "What do you say, Princess?"

She narrowed her gaze at him, but he could see the pulse booming at the base of her throat. Could hear the hitch in her breath when his attention strayed to her mouth—so perfectly pink.

"You weren't kidding about the pj's, were you?" she said, her voice suddenly unsteady. "You really do like them."

He ran his fingertips over her cheek. "Princess, where we're going, you won't need flannel."

He leaned closer, so close that her breath fanned across his lips and a surge of heat shot through him, so intense, so molten that he nearly groaned. What the hell was he doing? They were in the Stricklands' kitchen and he was on the verge of kissing her so hard and so deep that she'd forget all about the silly grudge her daddy had against his family.

"Is that a promise?" She lifted her chin ever so slightly, an invitation.

Finn's body hardened instantly. He didn't need to be asked twice. He could practically taste her already—perfectly tempting, perfectly sweet. All sugar and spice and everything nice.

She made a breathy little sound and it was nearly his undoing, but in the instant before his mouth came crashing down on hers, the door to the kitchen flew open.

"It smells delightful in here. Is breakfast ready?" Melba said.

Finn and Avery sprang apart like they were teenagers who'd just been caught behind the bleachers in high school.

"Yes. We were just about to come find you," Finn said, a blatant lie if he'd ever told one.

"That's exactly what it looked like you were about to do," Old Gene deadpanned.

Melba elbowed her husband in the ribs, and he flinched but shot Avery and Finn a wink when she wasn't looking.

Chapter Six

On Friday, Melba sat in the rocking chair on the shaded porch of the boarding house with the baby goat in her lap and eyed Avery's overnight bag.

"You're sure about going off alone for the weekend with Finn?" she said, looking mildly disapproving, as if she suspected that Avery's pajamas were still folded neatly in her dresser upstairs.

"Not the whole weekend." Avery held up a finger. "Just one night."

She had, in fact, packed her pajamas.

Because her night away with Finn at the B&B wasn't going to be about sex…not *all* about sex, anyway. The main reason she'd agreed to spend the night with him in the nearby town of Great Gulch was so she could finally tell him she was pregnant.

The secrecy had gone on long enough. It was past time she told him the truth, and she definitely couldn't go to bed with him until he knew about the baby…no matter how very badly she wanted to.

"Your room will be right here waiting for you when you come back." Melba shifted, and the goat let out one of her loud, warbly bleats.

"The little one sounds hungry," Avery said.

The little one.

Her throat grew dry.

"Doesn't she always?" Melba stood, and the tiny animal's cries grew louder.

"Hold on to her while I go get a bottle warmed up, will you, dear?"

"What? I... No..." Avery held up her hands in protest, but before she could come up with a reasonable excuse, she suddenly had an armful of kicking, squirming goat.

"I'll be right back." Melba pushed through the door into the boarding house, seemingly oblivious to Avery's distress.

She stared at the goat, and it stared back.

Meeeeeehhhhhhh.

"Shhh," Avery murmured. "Everything's fine, I promise. Or it will be as soon as Melba gets back."

The goat blinked its long eyelashes as if it was really listening to what she was saying. Its little ears twitched.

"You like it when I talk to you?" Avery smiled tentatively.

This wasn't so bad, really. It was sort of like holding a puppy.

Meeeeeehhhhhh.

"I know. I heard you the first time," she said, then turned at the sound of a car door slamming shut.

Finn grinned as he strode from his truck toward the front steps of the porch, a dimple flashing in his left cheek. "Now here's a sight I never thought I'd witness."

"What's that?" she asked, rocking slightly from side to side as the goat relaxed into her arms.

Finn arched a challenging eyebrow. "Corporate princess Avery Ellington holding a goat."

Right. The only thing that might be less likely was the sight of her holding a baby.

Oh, God.

She didn't even know what to do with a baby farm animal. How was she going to succeed as a single mother?

"You should take her." She thrust the

animal toward Finn. "I don't think she likes me."

"Don't be silly. Sure she does." He reached to scratch the goat behind one of her ears.

"You think so?"

"Yeah. You just need to relax a little bit." Finn shrugged, as if he'd just suggested the easiest thing in the world.

Relax…while holding a goat and pretending not to be secretly pregnant. No problem.

She took a deep breath. If a goat didn't like her, what hope would she have with a baby? Since the animal seemed to enjoy being rocked, she swayed softly from side to side. Seconds later, she was rewarded with a yawn and then some really sweet snuffling sounds.

"See? There's nothing to it," Finn whispered as the goat's eyes drifted closed.

To her embarrassment, Avery realized

she was blinking back tears. She sniffed. "Of course. Easy peasy."

Finn regarded her more closely. "Princess?"

She staunchly avoided his gaze, focusing intently on the goat's soft, ginger-colored fur with a swirl of white on its forehead. "Hmm?"

"Hey, talk to me." Finn brushed her hair from her eyes, the pad of his thumb coming to rest gently on the side of her face. "What's wrong? Are you having second thoughts about going to Great Gulch?"

"No, not at all." She shook her head. Second thoughts? God, no. She couldn't wait to spend time alone with him, except for the part where she needed to tell him he was going to be a father. But maybe that could wait just a tiny bit longer. "Nothing's wrong, I promise."

Liar.

No more waiting. She was getting weepy

over bonding with a goat. Finn clearly knew something was going on.

"Actually…" She cleared her throat. Maybe she should go ahead and tell him right here and right now. Just get it out. "I…"

"Oh, hello, Finn." Melba bustled out onto the porch with a bottle in her hand. She glanced back and forth between them. "I suppose you two are ready to head off on your…adventure."

Finn's lips tugged into a half grin. "Yes, ma'am. But do you want some help with that first?"

Avery went still as he reached for the bottle. What was he doing? She knew he was trying to stay in Melba's good graces, but surely she wasn't going to have to try to operate a baby bottle for the very first time while Finn and Melba watched.

"Be my guest." Melba handed him the bottle and reclaimed her place in the rocking chair. "Gene should be doing this himself, but as usual, he's found something else to do and left me in charge of this troublemaker."

"Do you want to do the honors, or should I?" Finn jiggled the bottle in Avery's direction.

Her heart jumped straight to her throat. She hadn't been this nervous since she'd taken her admissions exam before applying to graduate schools for her MBA.

Her panic must have been obvious, because Finn gently prodded the bottle's nipple toward the baby goat's mouth. "Like this, see?"

Within seconds, the goat was happily sucking at the bottle. Finn winked at her over the animal's fuzzy little head, and slowly, carefully he transitioned the bottle to her hand. Avery held her breath, but the switch didn't seem to bother the goat in the slightest. She felt herself grinning from ear to ear as the kid slurped up the rest of her formula.

"You're a natural," Finn said, and something about the sparkle in his warm brown eyes made her blush.

"That you are." Melba slipped her a curious glance. "You know what, dear? I think you're right. It's high time that wee one had a name."

"Oh, good." Avery handed Finn the empty bottle so she could set the goat down. Her hooves clip-clopped on the wooden planks of the porch. "What name did you choose?"

"I didn't." Melba shook her head. "I thought you might like to pick one."

"Me?" Avery's hand flew to her throat.

Melba shrugged. "If you'd rather not…"

"Pumpkin." It flew out of Avery's mouth almost before she knew what she was going to say.

"Pumpkin?" Finn laughed.

"It fits. Look at her." Avery gestured

toward the tiny animal, kicking and bucking up and down the porch steps on her little orange legs.

"I think it's perfect." Melba nodded. "Pumpkin, it is."

An hour later, Avery stood beside Finn as he slipped the key into their room at the bed-and-breakfast cottage in Great Gulch.

The tiny town was only about thirty miles from Rust Creek Falls, but it may as well have been in a different hemisphere. Avery hadn't spotted a familiar face since they'd crossed the county line, and after spending weeks in a place where everyone knew your name—and a fair amount of your personal business—it was a welcome relief.

She loved Rust Creek Falls. She loved Melba and Old Gene. She'd even developed a soft spot for Pumpkin, much to her own astonishment. But giving Finn such private news in a town where gossip was one of the local pastimes only added to her sense of dread about the whole thing. At least here if he reacted badly to the revelation that he was about to be a father, the only witnesses to his meltdown would be strangers.

But that wouldn't happen. Surely not. He'd been so sweet bottle-feeding the little goat. Avery could suddenly see him helping care for a newborn baby... loving his child.

Maybe even loving her.

"Here we are." Finn smiled down at her as held the door open.

Avery stepped into the room and gasped. A fireplace glowed in the corner of the room, bathing the space in glimmering gold light. The antique furniture was all crafted from dark cherry, the most spectacular piece being the four-poster bed covered in delicate lace bedding. Fairy lights were strung along the canopy, and an array of scented candles covered every available surface.

"Finn, this is lovely." She turned to face him, her head swimming with the rich, dreamy aroma of cinnamon and cloves mixed with something she couldn't quite put her finger on. Vanilla, perhaps.

"So you like it?" He dropped their overnight bags on a luggage rack beside a beautifully crafted armoire that looked like it might hold handmade quilts or chunky knit blankets.

"I love it. It's like something out of fairy tale," she said, suddenly wistful.

"Good." He studied her for a moment, and then his lips curved into a slow smile that gradually built into an expression that took Avery's breath away. "I've wanted to be alone with you, really alone, since the second I spotted you in the general store."

She let out a shuddering breath, and suddenly the air in the room felt thick with promise. Or maybe the intimate hush that had fallen between them was the memory of the night they'd spent in Oklahoma City.

"Avery." Finn held out his hand, and the subtext was clear. He wasn't just offering her his hand—he was offering her himself, body and soul.

But for how long?

She couldn't seem to move a muscle. Even breathing seemed difficult. Her heart was pounding so hard she thought she might choke.

Finn's face fell, and he dropped his hand. "Did I presume too much? If you don't want this…"

"I *do* want this. I want *you*…more than I can possibly say. This place, this room…it's all so beautiful. I don't want anything to mar our perfect night together." She inhaled a steadying breath before she hyperventilated. Why was this so hard? "I should have been straight with you from the start."

Finn closed the distance between them, wove his fingers through hers and kissed the backs of her hands. First one, then the other. Tenderly. Reverently. "Princess, there's nothing you can tell me that will change the way I feel about you."

She didn't deserve this kind of blind faith—not when she'd been hiding such an enormous secret from him.

"You can't know that," she said, shaking her head from side to side.

"I think I know what you're trying to say." He lifted a hand to her face, drawing his fingertips slowly across her cheek. She closed her eyes and fought the urge to lean into him. Because he couldn't possibly know, could he? "You came here on purpose looking for me."

She opened her eyes and nodded slowly. It was the truth, but not all of it. It was barely even the tip of the iceberg.

"That's great! I'm glad you did. Now come here." He wrapped an arm around her waist and pulled her close until she was pressed flush against him.

Then his mouth was suddenly on hers, and she was opening for him, wanting the warm, wet heat of his kiss—wanting it so badly she could have wept, because she could feel the crash of his heartbeat against hers. Frenzied. Desperate. And she could feel the way his body hardened as the kiss grew deeper, hotter.

Her fists curled around the soft material of his T-shirt, and in one swift move, Finn pulled back, slid the shirt over his head and tossed it onto the floor. In a heartbeat, he was kissing her again, cupping her face and groaning his pleasure into her mouth.

Avery's hands went instantly to the solid, muscular wall of his chest, and he felt so good, so right that she felt like she might die if he didn't take her to bed again. She'd wanted him since Oklahoma…since before she'd even known about the baby.

The baby.

Her eyes flew open and she pulled away, ending their kiss. Her palms, however, stubbornly remained pressed against his pectoral muscles. Was it her imagination, or had he gotten in even better shape since she'd last seen him shirtless? It must be all of the ranch work out at the Ambling A. It hardly seemed fair. He'd gone and made himself hotter while she'd been bursting out of her pencil skirts.

"Finn, wait."

He gave her one of his lazy, seductive smiles that she loved so much and glanced down at her hands, which seemed to be making an exploratory trail over the sculpted ridges of his abdomen. "We'll take it slow, baby. It will be good. So good."

She had no doubt that it would—better than the last time, even.

"We can't." She shook her head, somehow forced herself to stop touching him and crossed her arms.

Finn's gaze flitted to the bed and then back to her. "Why the heck not?"

She couldn't bring herself to say it. How could she? She couldn't even think straight while she was looking at that bare chest of his, much less form a coherent sentence.

But this was it—the moment of truth. One way or another, he was about to find out she was pregnant. He'd see the change in her body the second she undressed.

Slowly, she took his hand and rested it on her belly, telling him the only way she knew how.

His expression went blank for a moment, and then he stared down at his hand covering the slight swell of her tummy. The wait for understanding to fully dawn on him was agonizing. Avery lived and died a thousand deaths in that fraction of a second, until at last he lifted his gaze to hers. A whole array of emotions passed over his face, a lifetime of feelings all at once.

She took a deep breath. Then she let the rest of her secret unravel and laid it at his feet.

"It's yours."

Chapter Seven

Finn's ears rang.

The noise in his head started out as a faint roar—like listening to the inside of a seashell—but it multiplied by the second, drowning out all other sound. Avery's lips were moving, so he knew she hadn't stopped talking. But he couldn't make sense of the sounds coming out of her mouth. Nor could he hear the crackle of the fire in the old stone fireplace, even after he forced his gaze away from Avery and stared at its dancing flame.

He blinked, half tempted to stick his hand in the hearth to jolt himself back to life.

It's yours.

Avery was pregnant…with *his* child. He was going to be a father.

He didn't know whether to be furious or ecstatic. Somewhere beyond the scathing sense of betrayal, he was delighted at the news. A baby…with *Avery*.

That night in Oklahoma had changed him. Finn had realized that the moment he'd run into her at the general store. All the nonsense he'd put himself through since he'd moved to Montana—all the casual dates with women he didn't even know—reminded him what he was missing without Avery Ellington in his life. It was as if that Oklahoma City blackout had somehow split his life into two parts, before and after. Only now did he fully comprehend why it had felt that way.

But she should have told him sooner.

She'd been in town for *weeks* and hadn't said a word.

"It's mine," he said in an aching whisper. And with those two quiet words, the fog in his head cleared.

"Yes." Avery nodded, tears streaming down her face. "Yes, of course it's yours. There hasn't been anyone else. Not for a long, long time."

In the mirror hanging on the calico-papered wall, he saw himself shake his head. She didn't get it. Couldn't she understand? He wasn't questioning her assertion. He was stating a fact. The baby was his. *Theirs.*

Which meant he had a right to know of its existence.

"How could you have kept this from me all this time?" He closed his eyes and thought about all the times in the past few days he'd sensed that something was off. He'd *known*, damn it. He'd asked her time and again to tell him what was on her mind, and she'd refused. Every damn time.

"I tried to tell you. I really did. I just couldn't find the words. Please, you have to understand." She pressed her fingertips to her quivering mouth.

She stood stoically, awaiting his response. But he could see the hint of tension in her wide brown eyes, then he saw her bite her lip. And even in his fury, Finn hated himself for making her feel that way.

"I asked you to talk to me," he said with measured calmness. But his voice sounded cold and distant, even to his own ears. "I asked you what was wrong, and you looked me straight in the eye and said 'nothing.'"

He sat down on the edge of the bed and dropped his head in his hands.

"There were cows! And your father. And then I couldn't even bottle-feed the goat...and then..." The words caught. A sob escaped her, and when Finn looked up, Avery had wrapped her arms around her middle as if it took every bit of her strength to simply hold herself together. "Finn, I'm sorry. I didn't know how to tell you. I knew it would be a shock. It was for me, too."

He narrowed his gaze. What on earth was she rambling on about? Old Gene's orphaned goat?

She'd been so happy when the tiny thing took a liking to her. She'd beamed like she'd just won a shiny blue ribbon at the state fair. Was this what all that excitement had really been about? The baby?

Not the *baby*. Our *baby*.

"Look, I didn't even realize I was pregnant myself for quite some time. For *months*. I missed my period, and I was so tired all the time, I fell asleep at my desk! But I'd been working such long hours and I just thought…"

Finn flew to his feet. "Are you okay? Is the baby healthy?"

Avery nodded, her eyes still wet with tears.

What had he done? His first thought should have been about the baby, not how long it had taken her to tell him about the pregnancy.

He reached a trembling hand toward her belly and then pulled it back. He had no right to touch her. Not after the way he'd just spoken to her.

"Okay." He swallowed, shame settling in his gut. He couldn't turn back time and change his initial reaction, but he could still make this right. He *had* to make it right. "In the morning we will make the arrangements."

"The arrangements?" The color drained slowly from Avery's crestfallen face. "Surely you're not suggesting I have a… um…procedure?"

Over his dead body. She thought that much of him, did she?

"Princess, you really don't know me very well. Absolutely not." His gaze dropped to her belly again, and he had to ball his hands into fists to stop himself from reaching for her so he could feel the swell of life growing inside her.

The life they'd made *together.*

When he lifted his gaze back to hers, she regarded him with what looked like a cautious mixture of hope and shame. And he hated himself just a little bit more.

He was thoroughly botching this. It was time to make himself clear.

"You and I are getting married," he said flatly.

Avery's jaw dropped. She stared at him for a beat and then had the audacity to laugh in his face. "You can't be serious."

"As a heart attack," he said evenly.

No child of his was going to grow up

without a father. Finn knew all too well what it was like to be brought up without two present, supportive parents.

Maximilian was no saint. Finn wasn't fool enough to overlook the fact that his father could be manipulative and somewhat domineering. But he could count on one hand the number of times he'd seen his mother since she'd filed for divorce. She hadn't just walked away from her husband—she'd walked away from her six sons, too. An absence like that left its mark on a boy. A soul-deep wound that took a lifetime to heal.

Possibly longer.

Finn wouldn't do that to an innocent child. He would be there every step of the way, come hell or high water.

"Finn, what you said a few seconds ago is the truth. I don't really know you, and you don't know me, either. Certainly not well enough to entertain the idea of marriage." She shook her head and looked at him like he was as mad as a wet hen.

The only thing his impulsive proposal had accomplished was putting an end to her tears. That was something, at least.

"I won't be shut out of my child's life," he said. His voice broke, and something inside him seemed to break right along with it.

How had he and Avery come to this? They should be in bed together right now, but instead they were suddenly standing on opposite sides of the room as if the past few days hadn't happened at all.

Spending time with Avery in Rust Creek Falls had been fantastic, like something out of a dream. Finn had gone to bed every night thanking his lucky stars that she'd somehow found her way back into his life. He hadn't thought about his dad's ridiculous arrangement with Viv Dalton in days. He'd been too busy figuring out how to see more of Avery before she left town to think about the bounty on his head.

Oh, the irony.

Maximilian was going to be happier than a pig in slop when he heard about this. Avery's dad, not so much.

Just how much did her father despise the Crawfords? Finn hadn't given the matter much thought since he and Avery had agreed to put their family differences aside, but that would no longer be possible.

"I would never prevent you from seeing your child. You know how much I love it in Rust Creek Falls. I'll come visit, and you can come see the baby in Texas as often as you like," Avery said.

She took a step toward him, her hand resting protectively on the slight swell of her abdomen. She looked more beautiful than Finn had ever seen her before—already so attached to the baby they'd made together.

It seemed crazy, but Finn felt that way, too. Even though he'd only known about the pregnancy for a matter of minutes, an intimacy he'd never experienced before drew him closer to both Avery and their unborn child. Despite her words of assurance, a raw panic was clawing its way up his throat, so thick he almost choked on it.

He couldn't be just a visitor in their baby's life. He *wouldn't*.

"Can I ask you a question?" His jaw tightened, because he had a definite feeling he knew why Avery was so dead set on raising the baby on her own.

She blinked. "Of course."

He lifted a brow and fixed his gaze with hers. "How do your parents feel about the fact that you're carrying a Crawford heir?"

Because that's precisely what their child would be—an heir, not only to the Ellington fortune, but to everything the

Crawfords had built, as well. The two empires their fathers had created from the ground up would be forever intertwined in a way that neither of them had ever anticipated.

"Um." Avery looked away, and that's all it took for Finn to know the rest of the story.

Oscar Ellington had no idea that his darling princess of a daughter was pregnant with Finn Crawford's baby.

Avery felt sick, and for once, the slight dizziness and nausea that had her sinking onto the B&B's lovely four-poster bed had nothing to do with morning sickness.

She should have told Finn about the baby sooner. That much was obvious. If she could rewind the clock and go back to the very first time she'd seen him in Rust Creek Falls, she would blurt out the news right there in the middle of the general store. Melba would have fainted, and the news would have been all over town faster than she could max out her credit card during a Kate Spade sample sale, but that would have been just fine… because at least Finn would never have looked at her the way he was regarding her right now.

The look of betrayal in his dark eyes was almost enough to bring her to her knees. Her legs wobbled as she sat down, and a coldness settled into her bones, so raw and deep that a shiver ran up and down her spine. She felt more alone than she'd ever been in her entire life.

He wants to marry you, remember?

Weirdly, Finn's abrupt proposal—if you could even call it that, since it was more of a command than a question— only exacerbated the aching loneliness that had swept over her the minute he'd begun looking at her as if she'd inflicted the most terrible pain in the world on him. Probably because she knew his desire to get married had nothing to do with her. He wanted to be close to their baby.

Not her.

"My parents don't know I'm pregnant," she said, heart drumming hard in her chest.

She couldn't even look at Finn as she admitted the truth. When had she become such a coward? It was pathetic. Her baby deserved a mother who could face challenges head-on, like an adult. Not a spoiled princess who'd had everything handed to her on a silver platter.

She squared her shoulders and forced herself to meet Finn's gaze. "I'm going to tell them, obviously. But I wanted to tell you first."

The set of Finn's jaw softened, ever so slightly. But the hurt in his eyes remained.

Avery swallowed hard. "You deserved

to know before anyone else. You're the baby's father."

He took a deep breath, and she wondered what would happen if she went to him and wrapped her arms around him. Pressed her lips to his and kissed him with all the aching want she felt every time she looked at him.

Because she did still want him, and a part of her always would. They were tied together for life now. And as scary as that probably should have been, knowing her attraction to him was part of something bigger—something as meaningful as another life—gave her a strange sense of peace.

The only thing keeping her a chaste three feet away from him was stone-cold fear of what he would say or do next. He wanted to *marry* her, for crying out loud.

That was a hard no. This wasn't the 1950s. Besides, Avery wasn't about to marry a man who wasn't in love with her.

"Where do they think you are? You've been out of the office for weeks. I'm guessing you didn't actually have meetings in the area at all." Finn's brow furrowed, and he looked like he was mentally scrolling through all the little white lies she'd told since she'd rolled into town. She wanted to crawl under the bed's beautiful lace coverlet and hide.

He pinned her with a glare. She wasn't going anywhere.

No more hiding.

"There were no meetings." She shook her head. "Everyone—my mom and dad, the office—thinks I'm at a spa."

She waited for him to make a crack about what a completely believable lie that had been. Was there a soul on earth who would believe Princess Avery had been bottle-feeding a goat and carving pumpkins instead of munching on kale salad and getting daily massages at Canyon Ranch?

For once, he didn't poke fun at her, and for that, she was profoundly grateful. When he came and sat down beside her, she almost wept with relief.

But the feeling was fleeting, because he wasn't finished asking questions.

"I think it's high time your parents, especially your father, know what's going on. Don't you?" He turned to face her, and he was so close that she couldn't help but stare at him and wonder if her baby would have those same features.

Would he or she have those brown eyes with tiny gold flecks that she loved so much? The same nose? The same dimple that Finn had in his left cheek?

Her face went warm and she nodded. "Yes, I do."

If she was going to come clean, she might as well do a thorough job of it. Besides, telling Finn he was going to be a father had been the most difficult thing she'd ever done. As crazy as it seemed, the prospect of telling her parents seemed easy in comparison. Even talking to her father seemed manageable, especially with Finn sitting beside her.

They weren't an actual couple, and they *certainly* weren't getting married, but was it too much to think they could be something of a team where their baby was concerned?

He crossed the room to collect her handbag from the pile of their untouched luggage and handed it to her. "I'm assuming your phone is in here?"

She nodded. So this was happening now...as in, *right* now.

She could do this. She was a grown woman. Having a baby was a perfectly normal thing to do.

The phone trembled in her hand as she pulled up her parents' contact information, and Finn's gaze seemed to burn straight into her. She knew he fully expected her to chicken out, so she gave the send button a defiant tap of her finger.

The line started ringing, and she glanced at Finn for a little silent encouragement, but he stood in front of her with his arms crossed, stone-faced. Having him tower over her like that made her heart flutter even more rapidly, so she got up so they could stand eye to eye. Technically, they were eye to chest since he was so much taller than she was, but still. It helped.

The phone rang once, twice, three times. Then at last her father picked up. "Hello?"

"Daddy, hi," she said a little too brightly.

"Hello, sweetheart. Are you on your way back from the spa? I was beginning to wonder if you were ever coming home."

"No, not exactly," Avery said. Her gaze flitted again to Finn's serious expression, and she knew the time had come for the truth. All of it. "I actually haven't been to the spa. I've been in Montana."

There was a long stretch of silence before her dad responded.

"Montana," he said. "I don't understand."

"I'm in Rust Creek Falls." She didn't need to elaborate. Her father was well aware the Crawford ranch had picked up and moved away from Texas. He'd practically thrown a party.

Now his voice shifted from daddy mode to CEO mode in an instant. "Avery, what's going on?"

Before she could say anything, her mom picked up the other extension. "Avery? Hello? Are you okay? What's happened?"

Everything. *Everything* had happened. "I'm fine. I'm in Montana with Finn Crawford and, well, I have something I need to tell you."

Her eyes fixed with Finn's, and he took

her hand. It was the smallest possible indication that they were a united front, but
she seized on it as if it were a lifeline.

"We're having a baby," she blurted.

"Oh, dear," her mother said.

"What?" Oscar Ellington boomed. His
voice was so loud that Avery had to hold
the phone away from her ear.

"Daddy, calm down," she said, and
Finn's brows drew together in concern.

"I don't understand." Avery's mother
sounded mystified. "How did this happen?"

The usual way, Mom. Avery wasn't
about to get into the details. Her father
was already breathing loud enough to
make her wonder if he was on the verge
of a heart attack. "I'm four months along,
and I came up here to let Finn know."

"Is the Crawford boy there right now?
Put him on the phone," her father de-
manded.

The Crawford boy. What were they, twelve years old?

She gripped the phone tighter. "No."

Now wasn't the time for Finn and her dad to have a heart-to-heart, but this was probably the first time Avery had ever willfully refused her father...with the notable exception of sleeping with the enemy.

"Avery, I'm sending a private jet to collect you first thing in the morning. Be on it," her father said. Then he spat, "Alone."

"I can't leave so soon, Daddy. There are things I need to figure out here. But I'll be home soon."

"The hell you will," Finn said with deadly calm. "We're getting married, remember?"

Avery froze. Why in the world would he bring that up now?

She shushed him, but it was too late.

"Honey, I'm not sure getting married is the best idea," her mother said.

Her father was far more insistent. "Avery, I forbid you to marry that man. I won't have a Crawford anywhere near my business. The Ellingtons have the financial means to take care of a child without any help from him."

She wanted to explain that Finn wasn't the horrible person her parents thought he was, despite the fact that he was trying to strong-arm her into marrying him. He was decent. He was kind. Under different circumstances, he might have even been the love of her life.

But she couldn't say any of those things—not while Finn was right there listening to every word she said. She wasn't ready to put her heart on the line like that. Today had been a big enough disaster already. First and foremost, she needed to build a future for her baby.

Love was a luxury she couldn't worry about now.

Maybe not ever.

One thing was certain, though. She'd had enough of stubborn men telling her what to do. "Daddy, what exactly are you saying?"

He wanted her to hightail it back to Dallas, but somehow she sensed there was more.

She closed her eyes and concentrated on breathing in and out. No matter what her dad said, she couldn't board a private jet first thing in the morning. She and Finn still needed to hammer out custody arrangements. That might take a while, since he still seemed to think there was a wedding in their future, although she was sure Finn would change his mind once he had time to sleep on it. After all, he'd never much seemed like the marrying type.

Plus, Avery couldn't leave without telling Melba and Old Gene a proper good-bye. The thought of moving out of the boarding house suddenly left her with a lump in her throat. The Stricklands had been so kind to her for weeks now. And what about Pumpkin? She'd miss the sweet little goat.

Once you name an animal, it's yours.

Somehow she doubted her parents would welcome a baby goat any more than they'd welcome the news of her pregnancy.

"I'm telling you to come on home, Avery," her father said.

Just as she'd expected…

Almost.

"But only after you cut Finn Crawford out of your life entirely."

Chapter Eight

Finn felt his throat closing up as he watched Avery's eyes go wide and fill with tears again.

"Daddy, you don't mean that." Her voice was a shaky whisper.

Why had he insisted on the phone call with her parents? Oscar Ellington's disdain for Finn's family was clearly far worse than he'd imagined. So far Avery had done a remarkable job of standing her ground, but something had just changed. Finn wished he knew what.

"I can't deprive my baby of his father." Avery's gaze flew toward his. "It wouldn't be right."

Finn held out his hand. "Give me the phone, Avery."

He couldn't let this continue. She was getting too upset, too shaken. What if it somehow harmed the baby?

Finn wouldn't be able to live with himself if something terrible happened to either Avery or their unborn child all because he'd forced her to confront her parents.

"Avery, please," Finn said, working hard to keep his voice even and failing spectacularly.

At last she dropped the phone in his outstretched hand. "Too late. They hung up."

"Good." He tossed the phone onto the bed and jammed his hands on his hips.

"Good? Are you kidding?" She let out a hysterical laugh. "I just told my parents I'm having a baby and they hung up on me."

We, he wanted to say. *We* are having a baby.

Somehow he managed to bite his tongue. "The important thing is that it's done. They know."

She bit her lip, nodding slowly. "You're right. The worst is over. I'm sure my father will calm down after the news sinks in."

She didn't look sure. The fairy lights wrapped around the delicately carved frame of the romantic four-poster bed brought out the copper highlights in her hair, and Finn fought the urge to bury his hands in her dark waves.

He had the absurd wish that he could kiss her and make everything better. He wanted to lie beside her, take her into his arms and whisper promises that he knew good and well he couldn't keep.

It will all be okay.

Your parents will come around.
We're in this together.

He sat down beside her again, this time close enough for his thigh to press softly against hers. When she didn't pull away, he reached for her hand and wove their fingers together. Progress.

He gave her hand a gentle squeeze and dropped a tender kiss on her shoulder. She turned wide, frightened eyes toward him, but her lips curved into a wobbly smile. Maybe they really were in this together, after all.

He took a calming inhale and said, "We can start planning the wedding as soon as we get back to Rust Creek Falls."

Avery rolled her eyes and dropped his hand abruptly. "Would you stop with the wedding talk?"

And just like that, they were back at square one.

"It's not talk. I'm serious." He stood and started pacing from the bed to the fireplace and back again. "You're going to start showing soon, and everyone in town knows we've been seeing each other. I'll be damned if people start whispering that Finn Crawford has a bastard child. I won't do that to my baby. You shouldn't want that, either."

"You have no right to tell me what I should or shouldn't want. From what I hear, you've never been in any kind of committed relationship." She looked him up and down. "What makes you think you're so ready to jump into marriage?"

"What makes you think I'm not?" he countered.

"Oh, I don't know. Maybe the dozens of women you've dated since our night together in Oklahoma." She marched toward her suitcase while Finn stood, paralyzed.

Of course she knew about all those silly dates Viv Dalton had set him up on. No one could keep a secret in a town as small as Rust Creek Falls.

But it wasn't as if he'd been trying to hide anything. When he and Avery had parted ways in Oklahoma, they'd both thought they'd never see each other again—other than in the normal course of business. He'd done nothing wrong.

Then why did he suddenly feel like the biggest jerk in the world?

"Those women meant nothing," he said to her back as she gathered her luggage together. "I promise. If I told you the truth about why I'd been going on so many dates, you'd laugh."

She couldn't leave. If she walked out the door, she could be on the next plane to Dallas and he'd never know. He willed her to turn around and stay until they figured things out.

Together.

She dropped her suitcase with a thud

and spun around, arms crossed. "Try me. I could use a good laugh."

Finn drew in a long breath. "My dad wants all six of his sons married off. He's offered a matchmaker in town a million dollars—possibly more—to find wives for each of us. Those were all just meaningless setups."

Avery didn't laugh, but she didn't grab her suitcase again, either. A small victory.

Her eyes narrowed. "Because you didn't intend to marry any of them?"

"Exactly. I wasn't looking for a relationship. I was just…"

Having fun.

He couldn't say it, because he could suddenly see how the entire arrangement looked through Avery's eyes, and it certainly didn't seem like the actions of a man who was ready to marry anyone. Not even the mother of his child.

"Things are different now." He held up

his hands, either in an effort to stop her from fleeing or as a gesture of surrender. He wasn't sure which.

"Because I'm pregnant," she said flatly.

Was that the entire reason?

He wasn't sure, so he refrained from answering her. His head was spinning so fast that he couldn't make sense of his thoughts. Avery...a baby...a wedding. Was he ready for all of it?

"Right. That's what I thought." Avery nodded, taking his silence as an admission. "Let's table the marriage talk for now, okay?"

For now.

Finn's jaw clenched. Powerless to press the marriage issue again so soon, he felt an overwhelming emptiness gnaw at him as she continued.

"We can work out a generous visitation schedule while you and I get to know each other better." Avery smiled, but it didn't quite reach her eyes.

Where was that beautiful carefree woman who'd thrown her head back and laughed while one of his cows ate from her outstretched hand? Where was the light that always seemed to shine from somewhere deep within her soul?

Was the prospect of having a baby with him really so awful?

Perhaps, if they did it the way she was describing. She rattled off days of the week and alternating holidays in some crazy, mixed-up fashion that would require a spreadsheet to keep track of. She didn't bother mentioning the fact that if she went back to Dallas, a shared custody arrangement would require multiple flights across the country on a monthly, if not weekly, basis. Maybe it was a good thing her father had a private jet at his disposal.

The thought of Oscar Ellington made Finn grind his teeth so hard that he was in danger of cracking a molar.

"Avery, I…"

Before he could tell her he had no intention of shuttling an infant back and forth between time zones, her cell phone blared to life on the center of the bed. One word lit up the tiny screen: Daddy.

Avery scrambled to pick it up while Finn let out a relieved exhale. Thank God. Surely her parents had come to their senses and Oscar was calling to take back whatever awful things he'd said that had left Avery so shaken. She was the apple of her father's eye. His approval meant a lot to her, and once her dad had gotten over the initial shock, Finn and Avery could stop discussing the baby as if they were two complete strangers and get back to who they'd been in recent days.

And who's that exactly? The future Mr. and Mrs. Finn Crawford?

The thought did seem oddly appealing, despite the fact that he'd been doing everything in his power lately to avoid the altar.

"Daddy," Avery said, smiling faintly as she gripped her phone to her ear. "I'm so glad you called back."

Finn took a tense inhale and reminded himself that the supposed feud between their families wasn't an actual thing.

But apparently hatred was a powerful emotion, even when it was one-sided. Avery's face fell the moment her father started speaking. Finn couldn't make out what was being said, but whatever it was seemed to suck the life right out of her.

Avery's beautiful brown eyes settled into a dull, glassy stare.

"Daddy, be reasonable," she said. Then, in a voice choked with tears, "Daddy, that's not fair."

This time, when her father hung up on her again, she didn't appear panicked or angry or even sad. There was no spark of life in her expression whatsoever.

Her hands dropped to her sides, and the phone slipped from her grasp. It bounced off the toe of Finn's left cowboy boot and then skidded beneath the bed.

His gaze snagged on it as it disappeared from view, and when he looked back up, Avery's delicate face had gone ashen.

She shook her head as she blinked back a fresh wave of tears. "I've just been disinherited."

Avery lay in the dark, too exhausted to sleep. Too exhausted to do much of anything, really. Especially too exhausted to keep turning down Finn's marriage proposals.

What had gotten into him? It was as if finding out he was going to be a father had flipped a switch and transported him back to the 1950s. Hadn't he gotten the memo about modern families? Single mothers weren't unheard-of. Families took all shapes and forms nowadays. Just because she was pregnant didn't mean she needed a ring on her finger. She was perfectly capable of raising a baby on her own.

Or she would be, if she wasn't suddenly unemployed.

And homeless.

And alone.

Except she wasn't technically alone. Not entirely. Finn's long, lean form was stretched out beside her, looking more masculine than ever beneath the bed's gauzy white canopy. He'd kicked off his boots but otherwise remained fully dressed on top of the covers. After her big announcement, what was supposed to be a romantic getaway had turned into something much more somber. Any lingering flicker of romance had been fully doused by the most recent phone call from her father.

Now there might as well have been a

line drawn straight down the middle of the bed.

She and Finn hadn't discussed the fact that they wouldn't be sleeping together tonight. It had sort of been a given, though. Since she'd told him about the baby, that seemed to be the only thing they'd managed to agree on. Plus, nothing killed the mood like turning down a marriage proposal.

Avery bit the inside of her cheek to stop herself from crying again. Meanwhile, the father of her child was sleeping like a baby. Ugh, it was infuriating.

How could he rest so soundly while her whole world was falling apart? Probably because she was officially stuck in Montana.

He let out a soft snore, and she jabbed him with her elbow. The sharp poke managed to quiet Finn down, but he still didn't crack an eyelid. Avery briefly considered filling the ice bucket with cold water and dousing him with it, but honestly, a wide-awake Finn would be even worse than a snoring Finn at the moment.

She needed time to think. Time to figure out what to do now that she had nothing to return to in Dallas. In the span of one phone call, her entire life had gone up in smoke.

After she'd told Finn her parents had cut her off, they'd agreed to postpone any more baby talk until tomorrow morning. They'd eaten dinner in silence at a charming little bistro in Great Gulch and then returned to their gorgeous room in the B&B, where they'd been forced to deal with the awkwardness of sleeping in the same bed.

This isn't the way tonight was supposed to turn out.

Avery pulled the lacy comforter up to her neck and sneaked another glance at Finn. Was it possible to be thoroughly angry with a man and yet still want to curl up beside him and burrow against his shoulder? Because she sort of did.

She couldn't help it. It was ridiculous, she knew. But she'd spent the past week and a half wanting him like she'd never wanted another man, and those feelings were impossible to just turn off in an instant. She wished she could. Standing her ground on the whole marriage thing would be so much easier if her heart didn't give a little tug every time he mentioned it.

If she wasn't careful, she might make the critical mistake of falling for the father of her baby. That couldn't happen. She'd lost enough already—losing her heart to Rust Creek Falls' biggest playboy wasn't an option.

She took a deep breath and stared up at the ceiling. The twinkle lights draped from the bedposts bathed the pretty room in glittering starlight. Even in her despair, Avery got a lump in her throat at the beauty of it all.

Finn had chosen well. This would have been the perfect place to rekindle their physical relationship. It was like something out of a fairy tale, except instead of a happily-ever-after ending, she'd just been stripped of everything she'd always known and loved.

Disinherited.

She couldn't wrap her head around the concept. Never in her wildest dreams had she thought her family would turn its back on her under any circumstances, least of all these. She knew her father might be upset to find out she'd been intimate with a Crawford, but cutting her out of his life seemed especially cruel. And the fact that her mother was going along with it was wholly inconceivable.

Avery wasn't technically a mother yet, but she felt like one. In five short months, she'd be able to hold her baby in her arms. Right now, she didn't even know if she was having a boy or a girl, but that didn't matter. She loved her baby, sight unseen. She couldn't imagine ever shunning her child, no matter what. Wasn't that what love was all about—accepting someone unconditionally?

Maybe Avery had it coming, though. She'd been keeping such a big secret for far too long. Finn deserved to feel like a father every bit as much as she felt like a mother. Maybe getting disinherited was some cosmic form of punishment for failing to tell him the truth right away. It was probably a miracle that he wanted to have anything to do with her, much less marry her.

She swallowed around the lump in her throat. Finn wasn't such a terrible person. She knew that. He was a good man, just not exactly marriage material. He went through women like water, and his crazy explanation about why he'd been

dating so much was no comfort whatsoever. It made him seem more like a contestant on *The Bachelor* than ever.

And yet...

He was still there, right beside her,
when everyone else she knew and loved
had disappeared.

Which was why when the sun came
up the following morning, casting soft
pink light over the lacy white bedding
and bathing the room with all the hope
of a new day, Finn turned his face toward
hers and Avery whispered the precious
words he'd been waiting to hear.

"I'll marry you."

They were getting married.

After months of running away from the
altar as fast as he could, Finn was elated.
He, Avery and their child were going to
be a family. His baby would grow up
with a real father, one who was there for
him or her, every step of the way.

His relief was so palpable that it felt almost like something else. Joy. Maybe even...love.

He swept a lock of hair from Avery's face and pressed his mouth to hers. It was a tender kiss. Gentle and reverent, full of all the things he didn't know how to say. But while his eyes were still closed and his lips still sweet with Avery's warmth and softness, she laid a palm on his chest, covering his heart.

She didn't push him away, though. She didn't have to. He got the message all the same.

"I have a few conditions," she said.

Conditions?

His gut churned, and the sick feeling that had come over him last night as he'd watched Avery's agonizing phone calls with her parents made a rapid return.

He sat up. "Such as?"

Avery propped herself against the headboard next to him and crossed her arms. "For starters, I'd like to keep the pregnancy quiet for a while. Just between us, as long as I can continue getting away with baggy clothes."

He could live with that.

Finn nodded. "Fine. We can tell my family after the wedding. I'm not sure how quickly we can get the church, but once my dad hears we're engaged, I'm sure he'll be more than willing to pull a few strings and—"

She shook her head. Hard. "No."

"I'm not talking about an out-and-out bribe." Although Maximilian wasn't exactly a stranger to that type of behavior. "But we know people in town, and—"

She cut him off again. "I mean no church wedding. I'd like to keep things as simple as possible. A ceremony at the justice of the peace, maybe."

How romantic.

Finn suppressed the urge to sigh. After

all, they were getting married for the baby. Why did he keep forgetting that?

He reached for her hand and wove his fingers through hers. "Are you sure that's what you really want?"

"Yes, which brings me to my second condition." She glanced at their intertwined hands and then promptly looked away, taking a deep inhale. "Given the circumstances, I think a marriage of convenience is the best idea."

She let go of his hand and scrambled out of the bed, darting around the room as if she could somehow escape the remainder of the conversation.

No such luck, sweetheart.

"Avery," he said as calmly as he could manage. "What are you talking about?"

She began pulling things out of her suitcase, refusing to make eye contact with him. "I'm just saying that since this marriage is about the baby, we shouldn't muddy the waters by making it personal."

What could possibly be more personal than having a child together?

He arched a brow. "And by personal, I'm guessing you mean sex."

Avery's face went as red as a candy apple. "Exactly. I'm glad you agree."

He did not agree. In fact, he disagreed quite vehemently, but he wasn't about to push the matter.

She was scared.

Scratch that—she was terrified. And Finn couldn't really blame her. He'd always thought Maximilian Crawford was as tough a nut as they came, but clearly he'd been wrong. Avery's father made Maximilian look like a teddy bear.

"I want you to feel safe and secure," he said quietly. "I want that for our baby, too. And if that means no sex for the time being, that's fine."

"Actually, I—"

He held up a hand. "Let's take things one day at a time, okay?"

Surely she didn't think they were going to remain married for the rest of their lives and never make love. They were good together. So good. Once everything calmed down and they were living together as husband and wife, she'd realize he was in this for the long haul. She had to.

"One day at a time." She nodded and shoved her refolded items back into her suitcase. The poor thing was a nervous wreck.

Finn stood, raking a hand through his hair. "Why don't I go get us some coffee? Then we can get ready and head on down to the courthouse."

Her eyes grew wide. *"Today?"*

"Today." His voice was firm. "You have your conditions. This one's mine. There's no waiting period to get married in Montana. We just have to stop by a county office for a license and then we can go straight to the justice of the peace."

Thanks to his father's hobby as matchmaker extraordinaire, Finn knew more about getting married than he'd ever wanted to. For once, all the knowledge he'd picked up in Viv Dalton's wedding boutique was finally coming in handy.

Avery sighed. "Fine."

He crossed the room, intent on getting the coffee he'd mentioned. This conversation was really stretching the limits of his uncaffeinated early-morning state.

But as his hand twisted the doorknob, he paused. "Of course if you'd rather wait and have a church wedding in Rust Creek Falls, we can do that instead."

He could already see it—the little chapel at the corner of Cedar and Main all decked out in tulle and roses. A big fancy dress for Avery and all five of his brothers standing up for him at the altar. Maximilian with a triumphant smile on his face.

Funny how the thought of such a spectacle would have made him ill a month ago. Now, it actually sounded nice.

Maybe Avery was right. Maybe he didn't really know what he wanted.

"Nice try, but no." She let out a nervous little laugh and shook her head.

"All right, then. It's settled." He shoved his Stetson on his head and went out in search of coffee, bypassing the free stuff in the lobby in favor of something better.

He thought he remembered seeing a fancy coffeehouse a few blocks away as they'd driven into town. From the looks of the exterior, it had been the sort of place that served frothy, creamy drinks—lattes and cappuccinos with hearts swirled into the foam. Not his usual preference, but this morning it sounded about right.

After all, this was their wedding day.

Chapter Nine

It was all happening so fast.

Just a few hours ago, Avery had been sipping the cinnamon maple latte Finn had brought back for her—decaf, obviously—and now she was sitting in Great Gulch's justice of the peace court, waiting to officially become a Crawford.

The district clerk's office was situated just below them, in the building's basement. They'd been able to get their marriage license and then headed straight upstairs—one-stop shopping, so to speak.

With its rough-hewn wooden posts and quaint clock tower, the small-town Montana courthouse looked like something out of an old Western movie. The judge wore Wranglers and a cowboy hat, while the bailiff's boots jangled with actual spurs, as if he'd arrived at work on his horse and tied the animal to a hitching post right outside.

It was surreal and unique in a way that Avery was sure to remember, even though there was no wedding photographer to capture the moment. No maid of honor or best man. No proud papa walking her down the aisle.

She glanced at Finn sitting beside her in the same hat and snakeskin boots he'd worn on the drive from Rust Creek Falls the day before. He'd changed into a fresh shirt, and she'd found a lovely white eyelet dress with ruffled sleeves in one of the boutiques in Great Gulch's recently revitalized downtown district. Paired with turquoise boots—her "something blue"—she looked more like a Miss Texas contestant than how she'd ever pictured herself on her wedding day, but the wildflower bouquet that trembled in her hands was a colorful reminder that she was indeed about to pledge herself to Finn Crawford for as long as they both should live.

What am I doing?

Her father had disowned her less than twenty-four hours ago. Shouldn't she give him a chance to change his mind?

Then again, why should she? She'd never heard her daddy say a single nice thing about the Crawfords, so he wasn't likely to start anytime soon. And now that she was pregnant with Finn's baby, she'd crossed over to the dark side. There was no going back.

Still, was this really the answer?

"Avery Ellington and Finn Crawford." The judge looked down at the papers in front of him and then peered out at everyone seated in the smooth wooden benches of the courtroom's gallery. "Please step forward."

Finn glanced at her and smiled as he took her hand and led her toward the bench at the front of the tiny space.

Avery took a deep breath as she walked beside him, inhaling the rich scent of polished wood and the tiny fragrant blooms beyond the opened windows. Finn had told her the flowers were clematis, but most people called them sweet autumn. They climbed the courthouse facade in a shower of snowy white, giving the old building a dreamy, enchanted air, despite its dusty wood floor and the buffalo head mounted above the judge's bench.

Is this really happening?

Avery swallowed. This wasn't the way she'd always pictured her wedding.

Not that she'd been dreaming of getting married anytime soon. But didn't all little girls dream of their wedding day when they were young? Avery always thought she'd be married in a church, surrounded by friends and family. She'd wanted a white princess dress with a train, just like Kate Middleton. Like every other starry-eyed teen, she'd been glued to the television for the royal wedding back then. It seemed so perfect, a real-life fairy tale. Never once had she imagined herself tying the knot already pregnant and dressed like a cowgirl.

"Mr. Crawford and Miss Ellington." The judge's gaze flitted back and forth between them. "You're here to get married?"

Avery tried to answer him, but she couldn't seem to form any words.

Beside her, Finn nodded. "Yes, sir."

"I see you've got your license." Again, the judge sifted through his papers. Satisfied everything was in order, he removed his reading glasses and smiled. "Okay, then. Let's get to it."

Avery gripped her modest little bouquet with both hands as if it was some kind of life preserver. She felt like she might faint.

"We are gathered here in the presence of these witnesses to celebrate the joining of this man and this woman in the unity of marriage," the judge said.

Avery glanced at Finn, but he was staring straight ahead, so she couldn't get a read on his expression. Her pulse raced so fast that her knees were in danger of giving out on her.

It's not too late to change your mind.

No vows had been exchanged yet. She could apologize, turn around and walk right out of the courthouse. It wasn't as if anyone would stop her.

And then what?

She couldn't go home, but she wasn't completely helpless. She had an MBA, for crying out loud. Plus the Stricklands had become true friends. Maybe she could work out some kind of special arrangement to stay at the boarding house indefinitely. Surely she could pay them back eventually.

The more she thought about it, the more she liked the idea of staying with Old Gene and Melba. But if she walked away now, she and Finn would be over for good. There'd be no going back if she left him at the altar...even if the altar was technically a country courthouse with a shaggy buffalo head on the wall.

The judge droned on as her mind reeled, until finally he said, "Please face each other and hold hands."

The bailiff's spurs jangled as he stepped forward to take Avery's bouquet, prompting Finn to bite back a smile. At least he, too, seemed to appreciate the absurdity of the situation.

Once her hands were interlocked with

his, though, fleeing seemed like an exceedingly difficult prospect. Could she really bring herself to be a runaway bride when he was holding her hands and looking at her as if she was the most beautiful woman he'd ever seen?

Beneath the amusement dancing in his gaze, there was something else—something that stole the breath from her lungs. Something that made her wonder if the vows they were about to exchange were indeed just words.

She bit her bottom lip to keep it from trembling as the judge said something about marriage being one of life's greatest commitments and a celebration of unconditional love.

Her heart drummed. *Love.* Did she love Finn Crawford? Did *he* love *her*?

Of course not. This wasn't about love. It was about the baby. But a small part of herself wanted it to be real, and that realization scared the life out of her.

"Finn, do you take Avery to be your wife, to have and to hold from this day forward, for better or worse, for richer, for poorer, in sickness and in health, to love, honor and cherish until death do you part?" The judge looked expectantly at Finn, and the moment before he answered seemed to last an eternity.

"I do," he said, and there was a sincerity to his tone that made Avery's fear multiply tenfold.

It's not real, she reminded herself. *It's all just pretend.*

She could do this.

But *should* she?

She placed her free hand on her growing belly to anchor her to the here and now. But when the judge turned his tender gaze on her and began to recite the same question, her throat grew dry and what she suddenly wanted more than anything—more than the wedding she'd dreamed about as a little girl, more than knowing that her father would eventually come around—was a sign. Nothing huge, just a small indication that she was doing the right thing. Everything within her longed for it.

Please.

It was a crazy thing to ask. She knew it was, but she couldn't help wishing… hoping…praying.

And then the most miraculous thing happened. Beneath her fingertips came a tiny nudge. At first she thought she'd imagined it, but then it happened again. The second time it was firmer, more insistent. She looked down at her belly, stunned.

Oh, my gosh.

Her pretty dress fluttered the third time it happened, and that's when she knew for sure—her baby had just kicked. *Their* baby.

"Avery, sweetheart?" Finn prompted.

She looked up and found her husband-to-be and the judge both watching her expectantly, waiting for her to say something.

She inhaled a shaky breath, and for the first time since the awful phone call with her father, she felt like everything might just be okay, after all. She'd needed a sign, and she'd gotten one. A sign more perfect than she could have dreamed of.

She fixed her gaze with the man who'd just pledged to love, honor and cherish her in sickness and in health, for richer and for poorer, and did her best to forget that she was definitely the latter at the moment. She was completely dependent on a man she barely knew, a man who just might have the power to break her heart.

"I do," she whispered.

And against all odds, she meant it, because the moment the baby moved, she'd stopped playing pretend.

* * *

They'd done it. After spending the past few months actively avoiding the altar, Finn Crawford was a married man.

He bit back a smile as he maneuvered his truck off Great Gulch's Main Street and onto the highway that led to Rust Creek Falls. There was no logical reason for the swell of elation in his chest. He'd practically been forced to beg Avery to marry him, and according to her terms, the marriage was hardly something to celebrate. Finn had no doubt that if Oscar Ellington hadn't acted like the world's biggest jackass, his daughter wouldn't be wearing Finn's ring.

But there it sat on the third finger of her left hand—rose gold, with a stunner of a center stone. He'd bought it on impulse at an antiques store across the street from the B&B. Avery's eyes had grown wide when he slid it onto her finger in the courthouse, but she'd yet to ask him where it came from. Finn wasn't altogether sure whether her silence was a good thing or a bad one, but every so often he glanced at her in the passenger seat and caught her staring down at the ring, toying with it with the pad of her thumb.

Married.

The beautiful woman sitting beside him was his wife, and she was pregnant with his child. Overnight, he'd gone from being free and single to being a husband with a baby on the way. He should be terrified half out of his mind or, at the very least, somewhat concerned about Avery's sudden insistence on a chaste relationship.

So why wasn't he?

From the moment she'd looked up at him with tears in her eyes and whispered the words *I do*, he'd felt nothing but pure, unadulterated joy. He'd worry about the details tomorrow. For now, he was content to let himself believe that he was ready to be a family man.

"Where are we going?" Avery frowned at the scene beyond the windshield as the truck rolled into Rust Creek Falls. "You just missed the turnoff for the boarding house."

Was she serious?

"That's because we're not going to the Stricklands'. We're going to the Ambling A," Finn said quietly.

Avery said nothing, but instead of toying with her wedding ring, she hid her hand beneath the folds of her dress.

Finn tightened his grip on the steering wheel. "I want to introduce my family to my wife."

Avery blinked at him. *"Now?"*

"Why not? The baby will be here in a matter of months. They may as well get used to the idea."

She shook her head. "We're still keeping the baby news to ourselves for now, right? I'm concerned that once the news is out, it will be all over town."

Finn's shoulders tensed, but she had a point. One thing at a time. Plus, he'd already given Rust Creek Falls enough to gossip about since he'd moved to the Ambling A. If the busybodies in town knew Avery was pregnant, their marriage would be reduced to nothing but a shotgun wedding.

Isn't that what it is?

Yes…no…maybe.

He wasn't sure of anything anymore.

"Okay, we still won't say anything about the baby." He took a measured inhale. "For now."

"Good." Avery nodded, but she was visibly nervous as they turned onto the main road leading to his family's ranch. She wrung her hands until her knuckles turned white.

Finn wanted to comfort her, but he wasn't sure how, especially when he caught sight of the numerous vehicles parked in front of the massive log home. Maximilian's luxury SUV was situated in its usual spot, as was Wilder's truck. But four more automobiles were slotted beside them, which meant Logan, Xander, Hunter and Knox were probably up at the main house, as well. What the heck was going on? Were they having a party in his absence?

He shifted his truck into Park. "It looks like we're about to kill six birds with one stone."

Beside him, Avery closed her eyes and took several deep breaths. When her lashes fluttered open, she glanced at him and shrugged. "Yoga breathing. It reduces stress and anxiety. It's also supposed to be good for the baby."

Finn smiled, then took her hand and gave it a squeeze. He also decided right then and there that they couldn't spend their wedding night at the Ambling A.

Avery was right—they needed to be thinking about what was best for the baby. Staying under the same roof as his nutty father and the rest of his nosy family wouldn't be healthy for anyone, much less his unborn child. They'd get in, make their announcement and get out. Maybe they'd even head back to Great Gulch and that beautiful four-poster bed.

No sex, remember?

He sighed as he climbed out of the truck and slammed the driver's-side door shut. No sex. They had a deal. A completely ludicrous deal, but a deal nonetheless.

He had to give Avery credit—she put on a good show. When he pushed open the front door to the big log house, she greeted Maximilian with a big smile and a hug, just like a proper daughter-in-law. As luck would have it, not only were all five of his brothers situated around the big dining room table, but Xander's wife,

Lily, and Knox's other half, Genevieve, were there, too. Hunter's daughter, Wren, had a bandanna tucked into the collar of her T-shirt and was digging into a big bowl of chili. Logan's wife, Sarah, sat beside her, bouncing a giggling baby Sophia on her lap.

Finn's attention lingered on the happy nine-month-old, and his chest squeezed into a tight fist.

"Son? Everything okay?"

Finn blinked and dragged his gaze back to Maximilian. "Everything's fine. Great, actually. What's going on? I haven't seen the main house this full in a while."

"We're all about to head down to the fall festival for pumpkin bowling, so Lily put on a pot of chili first." Maximilian planted his hands on his hips. "A few of us tried calling you, but your phone rolled straight to voice mail."

Right. Because he'd been a little busy getting married and all.

"Pumpkin bowling?" Avery grinned. "That's a thing?"

Logan nodded. "Sure it is. It's like regular bowling, only with a pumpkin instead of a bowling ball. It's taking place on the big lawn at Rust Creek Falls Park, and Dad has grand plans to beat us all to smithereens."

"Not going to happen." Genevieve shook her head. "I've been practicing."

"Seriously?" Lily laughed.

"Oh, she's dead serious." Knox slung an arm around his wife and kissed the top of her blond hair. "G never kids about pumpkin bowling."

"Aunt Genevieve has been helping me, too," Wren said around a spoonful of chili. "She said we need to put Grandpa in his place."

"Oh, did she now?" Maximilian crossed his arms while the entire room collapsed into laughter.

"No worries, Dad. We have some news

that might take the sting out of the fact that the family has been conspiring against you." Finn slipped his arm around Avery's waist and pulled her close.

The room grew quiet until the only sound was the scraping of Wren's spoon against her bowl and the pounding of Avery's heart as she nestled against Finn's side. Only then, at such close range, could Finn tell that her smile seemed a bit strained around the edges. Forced.

Because after all, they were only pretending to be happy newlyweds. The only thing real about their union was the baby on the way.

"We're married," Finn blurted.

So much for finesse.

He'd intended to say something more poetic, but Avery's stiff smile was messing with his head. What had happened to all the heat that had been swirling between them since she'd thrown herself at him in the pasture? He couldn't look at an ear of calico corn anymore without feeling aroused. He wanted her so much it hurt. And he knew...he just *knew*...that Avery still wanted him, too.

"You're *what*?" Logan glanced back and forth between Finn and Avery.

"Wait. This is a joke, right?" Hunter let out a nervous laugh.

Xander and Knox exchanged stunned glances. Wilder and Hunter just stared, no doubt wondering if they must be next, considering that all of Maximilian's sons seemed to be falling like dominoes, one by one.

"Avery, sweetheart, is this true?" Finn's father set hopeful eyes on Avery. The pumpkin bowling conspiracy had apparently convinced him the entire family had it in for him. Probably because he deserved it after all the meddling he'd done in recent months.

Every head in the grand dining room swiveled in Avery's direction, and Finn's gut churned; he hoped against hope that none of his family members could see through the charade. He wasn't sure he could take it if they could, especially when Logan and Sarah, Xander and Lily, and Knox and Genevieve seemed so blissfully happy.

It was painful enough to know his wife didn't plan to share a bed with him, but it would be beyond humiliating for his brothers and his father to know it, too.

But in answer to Maximilian's question, Avery beamed up at Finn as if he'd hung the moon. Gazing into those warm brown eyes of hers took him right back to Oklahoma—the night that had changed both of their lives for good. And with a lump in his throat, he realized that if he could have gone back in time and done things differently, he wouldn't have changed a thing.

"It's true. Finn asked me to marry him last night, and we just couldn't wait.

We went to the justice of the peace this morning," Avery said, the perfect picture of a blushing bride, radiant with happiness. Finn would have sworn on his life she was telling the truth. "I'm a Crawford!"

Chapter Ten

I'm a Crawford.

The full consequences of what Avery had done didn't fully sink in until she said those words and watched Maximilian's face split into an ecstatic grin.

There was no turning back. The ring was on her finger, and now they'd shared the happy news with Finn's family. She was no longer Avery Ellington. She was Avery Crawford. *Mrs.* Finn Crawford.

"Well, I'll be." Maximilian let out a jubilant whoop that was so loud it shook the rafters of the extravagant log cabin his family called home. "Welcome to the family, darlin'."

He scooped her up in a big bear hug, and before she knew what was happening, Avery was being passed from one Crawford to the next, each one gushing with happiness over the surprise news. They were all so excited, so welcoming, that Avery had to remind herself that she wasn't truly a part of the family, despite the change in her last name. She and Finn were figuring things out, that's all. She'd married him to ensure that he would truly be a part of his baby's life, despite her father's attempts to cut him out entirely. He didn't honestly think of her as his wife, and she certainly wouldn't be standing in the grand main building of the Ambling A with Finn Crawford's ring on her finger if she weren't pregnant with his baby.

Her daddy would see things differently,

though. The fact that she'd traded the name Ellington for Crawford would be an unpardonable sin, regardless of the fact that she'd been disinherited. Oscar Ellington had put something terrible in motion when he'd cut her off, but nothing that couldn't have been stopped. One phone call—that's all it would have taken to undo all the pain he'd caused.

But this...

This couldn't be undone.

"I must say, I'm surprised." Wilder narrowed his gaze at Finn. "You swore up and down that wild horses couldn't drag you to the altar."

Avery's ribs constricted, but she glued her smile in place.

"Things change, brother," Finn said, and his gaze found hers and he sent her a knowing grin.

Things change.

Did they? Did they really?

"How adept are you at bowling, Avery?"

Genevieve arched a brow. "Do you have much experience handling pumpkins?"

Finn shook his head. "Don't get any ideas. The lot of you already outnumber Dad by a good amount. You're going to have to trounce him on your own."

He reached for Avery, and his fingertips slid to the back of her neck, leaving a riot of goose bumps in their wake. "Besides, it's our wedding night."

Her stomach immediately went into free fall.

Their wedding night? She hadn't thought that far ahead. Since telling Finn about the baby, she'd pretty much been operating on a minute-by-minute basis.

"Won't you two be taking a honeymoon? I can make a phone call and get the jet down from Helena in two shakes of a lamb's tail." Maximilian dug around in the pocket of his Wranglers for his cell phone.

"Oh, there's no need for that," Avery

said before Finn could take him up on the offer. "We're not taking a honeymoon quite yet. Right...darling?"

She cast a pleading glance at Finn.

Darling? She was calling him darling now?

The corner of his mouth quirked into a half grin. "Right, love."

Love. As endearments went, it was a good one. A great one, actually. She practically melted into a puddle right there in the Crawford dining room, because again, she couldn't quite keep track of what was real and what wasn't.

"Maybe it's a good thing we're all heading out, then." Knox bit back a smile.

"Don't be an idiot. We're waiting on the honeymoon, but we're not spending our wedding night under the same roof as all of you." Finn rolled his eyes and punched his brother on the arm.

Knox winced as he rubbed his biceps.

"Point taken, but where exactly are you going?"

Finn hesitated, because as Avery knew all too well, he was completely winging it. It was the briefest of pauses, but it gave Maximilian the perfect opening to swoop in with a grand, romantic gesture.

"You'll stay at Maverick Manor. The honeymoon suite!" He jabbed at the screen of his cell phone. "I'll take care of the reservation myself, pull some strings if I have to."

Panic shot through Avery. She couldn't spend the night with Finn in a *honeymoon suite*, of all things. Not if she had any chance of sticking to the arrangement they'd made.

"What's Maverick Manor?" she asked, even though she dreaded the answer.

"It's Rust Creek's newest hotel. Rustic, but upscale." Hunter grabbed a coffee carafe from the marble-topped kitchen counter where a huge blue Le Creuset enamel pot sat, surrounded by bowls of chili fixings. He gave a thoughtful shrug while refilling his cup. "It's quite beautiful, actually. The lobby has a stone fireplace that's so big you can stand upright in it, and the entire back side of the building faces the mountains."

"It's so romantic, Avery. Honestly, it's the perfect place for a wedding night." Sarah sighed. "You'll just love it."

Avery glanced at Finn—at his big broad shoulders, at his capable hands, at the mouth she couldn't seem to stop kissing at the most inappropriate times. Then she shifted her attention back to her father-in-law, grinning from ear to ear.

What bride would turn down the honeymoon suite at the most extravagant hotel in town?

A pretend one. That's who.

Avery was suddenly exhausted. She'd been married all of two hours, and reminding herself not to fall in love with her husband was already becoming a full-time job. Maybe it was a good thing she was unemployed.

"Thank you, Maximilian. That's so kind of you." She took a deep breath. How hard could it be to spend one chaste night in a luxurious room with Finn? It wasn't as if the bed would be heart-shaped. Would it? "Maverick Manor, here we come."

Avery had no idea what Maximilian had said to the staff at Maverick Manor, but whatever it was had everyone falling all over themselves to welcome her and Finn in grand romantic fashion.

"Congratulations, Mr. and Mrs. Craw-ford," the front desk clerk gushed the in-stant they'd set foot inside the lobby.

They hadn't even introduced them-selves, which had Avery wondering if Maximilian had gone so far as to send photos in preparation of their arrival.

Finn's father was definitely over-the-top, so she wouldn't put it past him. Then again, Rust Creek Falls was a small town, and everyone within a one-hundred-mile radius seemed to know precisely who Finn Crawford was...because they'd dated him at some point.

Avery forced a smile and tried not to imagine the effusive blonde with the Maverick Manor badge pinned to her cute denim dress sharing a candlelit meal with her husband.

"We've prepared a lovely stay for you," she said, and to her credit, she didn't seem overly familiar with Finn. *Thank goodness.* She must be new in town. "Tomorrow, we've got you booked for a special couples' massage overlooking the fall foliage on our new pool deck."

"A couples' massage?" Avery blinked. Apparently, a heart-shaped bed was the least of her worries. "That won't be necessary. We're checking out tomorrow morning."

"Are you sure, love?" Finn's hand slipped onto the small of her back, and a rebellious shiver snaked its way up Avery's spine.

"A couples' massage sounds quite—" his gaze flitted toward hers, eyes molten "—nice."

Avery knew that look. It was a look full of heat and promises. The same playfully wicked expression that she'd loved so much that night in Oklahoma. What woman wouldn't?

Damn him.

"Mr. Crawford booked the honeymoon suite for a three-night stay," the clerk oh, so helpfully said.

"If only we could stay that long." Avery batted her lashes at Finn, whose hand remained on her back, where it continued to infuse her with the sort of warmth she most definitely didn't need to be experiencing at the moment. "But we have an appointment tomorrow morning that we simply can't miss. Don't we, darling?"

They did, actually. Finn just didn't know it yet.

He angled his head toward her. "We do?"

Avery's first official prenatal appointment with an obstetrician was scheduled for the following morning at eleven o' clock. Her gynecologist back in Dallas had started her on prenatal vitamins once her pregnancy test had come back positive, but since she no longer delivered babies, she'd given Avery a referral. After a few days in Rust Creek Falls had turned into a week and a week into two, she'd finally broken down and found a doctor in Montana. She'd made the appointment last week, before Finn knew anything about the baby, so she'd chosen a doctor whose practice was situated a half hour away from Rust Creek Falls. That still seemed like a good call, since being in such a small town was like living in a fishbowl.

"Yes, we do." Avery nodded, hopefully putting a firm end to the idea of a couples' massage.

"So, just one night, then?" The clerk glanced back and forth between them.

"Just one night," Finn said with a sudden hint of regret in his gaze that seemed so real that Avery felt it deep in the pit of her stomach.

What were they *doing*?

"Well, the staff at Maverick Manor is here to help you make the most of it. Just let us know if you need anything. Anything at all." The clerk handed two keys to an attendant who looked like he'd arrived fresh off the rodeo circuit. "Kent here will show you to your room."

The congratulatory glint in her eye turned wistful, and it was then that Avery knew the young woman had indeed been one of Finn's many Friday night social engagements. Not to mention the other six days of the week.

She felt sick as she followed Kent, with his perfect felt Stetson and worn cowboy boots, to the top floor of Maverick Manor. The minute Melba had warned her about Finn's overactive social life, she should have turned tail and gone back to Dallas. She could have left him a note about the baby or written him an email. That would have been the chicken's way out, obviously, and Finn would have no doubt beaten an immediate trail to Texas. But at least then she would have been on her home turf. She might have stood a chance at escaping from their one-night stand with her dignity—and her heart—intact.

Now here she was. In Montana, of all places, with a wedding ring on her finger and her heart in serious danger of cracking into a million pieces.

"Here we are." With a flourish, Kent gestured to the intricately carved door at the end of the hall. Then he unlocked it and held the door open, waiting for the "giddy" newlyweds to step inside.

A heady wave of fragrance drifted from inside the sumptuous room— something floral and sweet. Hyacinths, maybe. They'd always been Avery's favorite flower. And were those *rose petals* strewn on the floor?

God help her, they were. Where was a dust buster when she really needed one?

Avery stared at the petals, terrified to move. As luck would have it, she didn't need to, because before she could register what was happening, Finn scooped her in his arms and swept her clear off her feet.

She squealed in protest, even as her arms wrapped instinctively around Finn's thick neck. He laughed and it vibrated through her, sweet and forbidden.

Avery buried her face in the crook of his neck and whispered again the warmth of his skin. "What are you doing?"

"How would it look if I didn't carry my bride over the threshold? Just go with it, love," he murmured.

They were going to have words about this. They were also going to have words about his new nickname for her, because yes, they needed to put on a good show so their marriage was believable to the outside world, but she was only human. She had feelings, and right now, those feelings were in serious danger of throwing caution to the wind.

She blamed biology. Wasn't she chemically programmed to be attracted to the father of her baby?

Right. That's it. Science. It has nothing to do with his easy sense of humor or how sweet he is around animals or his generous spirit.

Or how he'd turned his entire life inside out for the sake of their baby. Or how he'd been there for her at a time when her own family had turned their backs on her. Or how he looked at her as if he'd simply been biding his time with all those other women, waiting for her to walk back into his life.

The list went on.

And on.

And on…

Kent tucked their bags away in the closet by the door and slipped out of the suite, yet Avery's feet still weren't touching the ground. The heat in Finn's gaze was suddenly infused with a tenderness that made it difficult to breathe. She looked away, determined to collect herself, but it was then that she noticed the trail of rose petals led to a huge bed covered in pristine white bed linens, facing a picture window with a stunning view of the mountains. The sun was just beginning to dip low on the horizon, bathing the yellow aspen trees in glittering light. Their leaves sparkled like pennies, and it was all so beautiful that Avery had to squeeze her eyes closed against the romantic assault on her senses.

When she opened them, she found Finn watching her...waiting. Was he ever going to put her down?

"If you make a crack about my weight right now, I'll never forgive you." She gave him a tremulous smile.

It wasn't a test. She was merely trying to inject some humor into a situation that suddenly seemed far too intimate. Had it been a test, though, Finn would have passed with flying colors.

"I wouldn't dare." His gaze narrowed and swept over her face, settling on her mouth. "You really have no idea how lovely you are, do you? Pregnancy suits you."

She had a sudden flashback of Finn moving over her, looking at her with the same reverence in his eyes as he pushed deep inside her, whispering sweet nothings. At the time, she'd attributed his words to the martinis and the darkness of the blackout, which had a strange way of making everything feel more real, more intense.

But maybe she'd been wrong. Maybe he really had felt those things. Maybe he still did.

"Thank you," she said stiffly, scrambling out of his arms and sliding clumsily to her feet. She took a giant backward step and pretended not to notice when Finn's expression closed like a book. "I'm kind of tired. I should probably get some rest."

"Right. Maybe we should take a nap." He scrubbed at the back of his neck and seemed to look anywhere and everywhere—except at her. "On top of the covers. Fully clothed."

This was the moment when she should

have told him the truth—the moment she should have given up the pretense that she didn't have feelings for the father of her child. It would be so easy. She might not need to say anything at all. She could just rise up on tiptoe and kiss him gently on the mouth, and he would *know*. He probably already did.

But she couldn't do it. She couldn't open herself up that way. The past twenty-four hours had been more heartbreaking than she could have ever imagined. She'd lost her job. She'd lost her family. She couldn't lose Finn, too, and that's precisely what would happen if she tried to start something real with him and then realized he didn't love her. If he did, wouldn't he have led with that when he asked her to marry him?

"That sounds good." She nodded. Could this honeymoon get any more awkward? "I have a doctor's appointment tomorrow, at eleven if you'd like to come along. For the baby."

"For the baby," he echoed, and his tone went flat. Lifeless. "Of course I'll be there."

She nodded, because she didn't quite trust herself to speak.

"You okay, Princess?" Finn said, a bit of life creeping back into his tone.

"Yes." She nodded. "Just tired."

So very tired. Tired of dealing with her impossible father, tired of wondering what kind of mother she would be, tired of acting like the night in Oklahoma hadn't meant anything when just the opposite was true. But most of all, she was tired of pretending. Sometimes it seemed like that's all she'd been doing since the day she rolled into Montana—pretending she wasn't pregnant, pretending she didn't have feelings for Finn, and now, pretending they were like any other husband and wife. Suddenly, with Finn's ring on her finger, she wasn't sure she could do it anymore.

"Come on." Finn strode to the bed and gave the mattress a pat. "Lie down. I promise I won't bite."

He smiled, but somehow it was one of the saddest smiles Avery had ever seen. So she did as he said, kicked off her boots and curled onto her side on the bed with her hands tucked neatly beneath her pillow, lest they get their own improper ideas.

Her eyes drifted shut and just as she began to doze off, she felt the mattress dip with the weight of Finn's body. So solid. So strong.

Tears pricked her eyes, and she wasn't sure why she was crying. She only knew that it was almost physically painful to have him so close without actually touching her. The space between them felt heavy, weighted with all things they couldn't say or do to one another.

When they'd been together in Oklahoma, they'd fallen onto the bed together in a tangle of kisses and heated breath. Despite the martinis, she remembered everything about that night with perfect clarity. The thrill that coursed through her when she'd slid her hands up the back of his dress shirt. The way Finn's eyes had gone dark when looked at her bare body for the first time. His aching groan when he'd pushed his way inside her.

She remembered it all as clearly as if it had just happened yesterday. Did he remember, too?

Was he thinking about it right now, just as she was?

"Princess?" Finn's voice cut through the memories, but the ache in his tone was all too familiar. Too tortured to leave room for any doubt.

Of course he remembers. Of course he's thinking about it.

All she needed to do was turn to face

him. She wouldn't even have to say anything. Everything she felt would be clearly written in her eyes—so much longing, and despite the craziness of their circumstances, so much hope.

She bit down hard on her lip to keep herself from answering him. And she didn't dare move. Instead, she squeezed her eyes shut tight and kept her back to her husband.

Then Avery Crawford let the heavy silence and the sweet smell of velvety rose petals lull her to sleep.

Chapter Eleven

Hours later, Finn lay stretched out on the sofa and stared at the ceiling, fully awake. He was either too mad or too turned on to sleep. Probably both, but he couldn't seem to figure out which bothered him most.

Avery wanted him. He knew she did, but something was holding her back. He just couldn't figure out what that *something* was, and he didn't want to push. She was his wife now, and she was pregnant. The burden of patience definitely fell on his shoulders in this scenario, hence his move from the bed to the sofa.

But they'd shared a moment earlier. He thought they had, anyway.

He glared hard at the rough-hewn wood beams overhead, wishing he could ask the room for confirmation. The space itself was glorious, with one wall completely made of stone opposite floor-to-ceiling windows overlooking the rugged Montana landscape. A fire blazed and crackled in the hearth. Hours ago, the air had been thick with longing, and now...

Now, nothing. Surely the walls remembered. Finn sure as hell did.

He sat up and raked his hand through his hair, tugging hard at the ends. Then he sighed, because in that moment, sleep seemed like the most impossible task in the world. He'd be better off spending half an hour under the cold spray of the suite's luxury rainfall shower head than continuing to lie on the sofa listening to the steady breath of his wife as she slept like a baby in the huge four-poster bed. Alone.

He stalked toward the closet, grabbed his duffel bag and slipped as quietly as he could into the grand his-and-hers bathroom. Through his sock feet, he could feel the warmth of the heated stone floor tiles. A Jacuzzi tub overlooked the darkening Montana sky, and like everything else in the suite, the enormous stone shower was built for two. He didn't need to close his eyes to dream of Avery, bare and beautiful, with water streaming down her changing body and droplets glittering on her eyelashes like stars. Sometimes it seemed as if she was all he saw, day or night.

It was making him crazy. They just needed to go ahead and sleep together so they could both get it out of their systems. Then they could go about dealing with the pregnancy with level heads. At least he hoped that's what would happen, because he wasn't sure how much longer he could go on the way things were.

Finn wasn't used to being so wrapped up in a woman like this. He was operating in strange and new territory, and he wasn't sure what to make of it. The baby had changed everything. Obviously.

Although...

Avery had been on his mind ever since Oklahoma, long before he had any idea she was carrying his child. On some primal level, he must have known. It was the only explanation.

The only one he was comfortable admitting to himself, anyway.

Get yourself together.

He glowered at his reflection in the bathroom mirror and hauled his duffel onto the natural marble vanity top. He'd been in such a hurry back at the Ambling A that he'd grabbed the first few articles of clothing he'd seen and stuffed them into his overnight bag along with his dopp kit. He wasn't even sure what all he'd brought.

But he was certain he hadn't packed the jewel-encrusted book that rested on top of his belongings and caught his eye the moment he drew back the zipper on his bag. He picked it up, turning it over in his hands. It was studded with colorful gemstones and looked like something he might see in the windows of one of the antique shops downtown. The jewels formed a swirling letter *A* on the front cover.

He squinted at it. The book definitely looked familiar, but how had it managed to get inside his bag, and what was he supposed to do with it?

Knox.

Finn sighed. He'd thought it was strange when his newlywed brother had insisted on carrying his bag to the truck so Finn could help Avery with her things. He definitely could have managed all their luggage on his own. But apparently Knox's helpful attitude had been a ploy to get his hands on Finn's duffel so he could tuck the book inside. Now that he knew where the gaudy thing had come from, he recognized it as the old diary that he and his brothers had found beneath the floorboards of the Ambling A when they'd been renovating the place a few months ago. Someone had finally managed to pry the lock open—Xander, if Finn was remembering correctly—and since that time, the old book had been making the rounds as each of his brothers had gotten married. Knox had been the most recent to walk down the aisle, so it made sense that the diary would still be in his possession.

Seriously, though? He was supposed to spend his wedding night reading an old book?

It's not like you're busy doing anything else at the moment.

True. So frustratingly true.

His jaw clenched as he moved to sit down, taking the book with him. Mildly surprised to find that the author was a man, he kept reading.

Oddly enough, the diary proved to be a pretty effective way of getting his mind off Avery and the myriad ways he'd rather be spending his wedding night than sitting on the bathroom floor with his legs stretched out in front of him, poring over the details of some poor sod from a different era. But as fate would have it, the author's girlfriend had been pregnant.

A child. A child! Unexpected, unplanned, but not for a moment unwanted. From the second I learned I was going to be a father, nothing else mattered. Only her—only the mother of my baby and the life we're bringing into the world.

Finn's pulse kicked up a notch when he came across that notable detail. And his heart seemed to make its way to his throat as he read passage after passage about how happy the writer was about the baby. The writer never spelled out his girlfriend's name, but referred to her simply as W throughout the book. As Finn slowly flipped the pages, he realized why.

All this time...all these days we've lived and loved in secret. And now we can't tell anyone about the baby. Not yet. So we continue to go through life pretending, but it's getting more difficult by the hour. W is my whole heart, and I want the world to know how much she and our child mean to me. But as we both know, it's just not possible. Not now. Maybe not ever...

W and her sweetheart were keeping the pregnancy and their relationship under wraps for some reason. He wasn't sure why, but they wanted to keep the baby a secret.

That's when Finn slammed the bejeweled book closed. The similarities were beginning to freak him out a little bit. He felt for the poor guy and W, whoever they were. He really did, but most of all, he wasn't sure he wanted to know how their love story would end.

Avery slept like the dead. The turmoil of the past forty-eight hours had taken its toll, and once her head hit the pillow, she was finally able to escape the craziness that was now her life. She woke the next morning to sunlight streaming through the suite's massive picture window and a scowl on her husband's face.

"Oh." She winced as she sat up and caught her first glimpse of Finn slumped on the sofa. He was already fully dressed, cowboy boots and all. "Did you sleep at all last night?"

Finn looked terrible. He was still the same handsome man who had the annoying habit of making her heart swoop every time she looked at him, but there were new dark circles under his eyes. Even the heavy dose of fresh scruff on his jaw couldn't hide the fact that his complexion was a good shade or two paler than normal.

"Good morning. I'm fine, don't worry about me." His voice was stiff as he closed the strange jeweled book in his hand. "I got you some coffee. It's decaf, so it should be safe."

He nodded toward one of the nightstands flanking the bed, where a steaming latte sat waiting for her with a heart swirled into the foam, and her guilt magnified tenfold.

He really should have stayed in the bed last night. For goodness' sake, it was so large that they each could have easily spread out like starfish and still not even touched one another.

Maybe.

Then again, maybe not. The last time she'd slept all night in a bed with Finn, she'd woken up convinced that she should marry him.

"Thank you." She reached for the latte and took a sip. Pumpkin spice, her favorite. She could still manage to drink it even though the smell of coffee beans sometimes made her nauseous.

But what didn't make her nauseous these days?

Finn stood and tucked the book he'd been reading into his duffel bag, then shifted awkwardly from one booted foot to the other. "You said your doctor's appointment is at eleven, right?"

She nodded.

He picked up his duffel, jammed his Stetson on his head and strolled toward the door. "We should leave in half an hour. I'll wait for you downstairs."

And then with a quiet click of the suite's carved wooden door, he was gone.

Okay, then. Clearly it hadn't been a magical wedding night.

But she'd been clear about the terms of their marriage from the very beginning. She didn't have a single thing to feel guilty about. Well, other than Finn's serious case of bedhead this morning and the fact that she felt perfectly rested. And maybe, just maybe, that she'd basically run for cover the night before at the first hint of sexual tension between the two of them.

That had been a very necessary moment of self-preservation, though. Surely Finn would get over it. He couldn't stay grumpy forever, could he?

Avery bathed, dressed and met Finn downstairs in half an hour, as requested. He smiled politely at her, carried her luggage and helped her into the truck, but something still seemed off. Despite every effort to dote on her, Finn barely looked at her. Avery should have been thrilled. After all, this was exactly the sort of arrangement she'd wanted. No risk. No pressure. No sex.

Absolutely no sex.

Yet she felt strangely hollow as they drove to her doctor's appointment. When they hit the open highway and Finn relaxed beside her, dropping his right hand to his thigh, she had to stop herself from reaching for it and weaving her fingers through his. She'd grown accustomed to his touch over their time together, and it felt strange now to be so close to him without feeling the brush of his skin against hers. She missed it more than she wanted to admit.

Be careful what you wish for.

The thought spun around and around in her mind as they wound their way past clusters of trees in saffron yellows and fiery reds. Bear's Paw, the town where her obstetrician was located, was situated halfway between Rust Creek Falls and Billings—close enough to a major medical facility in case something went wrong with her pregnancy, but still remote enough to guarantee a modicum of privacy. Avery only hoped Finn had never dated anyone who worked at the practice.

For the first time since their epic argument in Great Gulch, she considered what Finn had told her about his father's efforts to find brides for all six of his sons, to the tune of a million dollars. It sounded crazy. Then again, Maximilian Crawford was definitely the sort of man who got what he wanted, regardless of the cost.

Perhaps she shouldn't be so quick to judge Finn for systematically dating his way through the eligible female population of Montana. As he'd said, they'd been nothing but meaningless setups. Somehow, though, that almost made it worse. He'd been so intent on proving he couldn't be dragged to the altar that he'd acted like a kid in a candy store. And now here he was, right where he'd never wanted to be. Married.

She couldn't help but feel like the consolation prize. And still, all she wanted right then in the world was to hold his hand. Unbelievable.

"Almost there." Finn glanced at her, but his smile was stiff as he exited the highway and turned onto Bear Paw's quaint Main Street.

The town square, with its white gazebo in the center and surrounding mom-and-pop businesses, reminded Avery of both Great Gulch and Rust Creek Falls. There was certainly no shortage of small-town charm in Montana. Raising a family here would be so different than it would in a big city like Dallas. The thought put a lump in Avery's throat, and she wasn't sure why.

Finn's truck slowed to a stop in front of a redbrick building with an arch made of antlers hanging over the entryway.

"Here we are." He nodded.

"Yes, here we are." There was a telltale waver in her voice that had Finn's gaze narrowing in her direction.

For the first time since the night before when she'd leaped out of his arms, he looked at her...*really* looked.

"Hey." He cupped her face in one of his big, warm hands, and the simple contact was such a relief that Avery nearly wept.

Was she in for another five full months of out-of-control emotions? Because it was really getting old.

"You're not nervous about this, are you?" Finn said as his thumb made gentle circular motions on her cheek.

She was most definitely nervous about seeing the doctor. Terrified, actually.

Despite her recent success with the baby goat, she had no clue what she was doing. She'd been such a mess lately. What if the stress of keeping the pregnancy a secret from Finn for so long had somehow harmed the baby?

She'd never forgive herself if that were true. "I'm a little nervous."

"Listen to me." He leaned his forehead against hers, and as his gaze fixed with hers, the new frostiness between them thawed ever so slightly. "Everything is going to be fine. Okay?"

She nodded. "Okay."

With Finn there, it seemed easier to believe. And if anything was indeed wrong, at least she wouldn't have to handle it all on her own.

Her chest grew tight as she climbed out of the truck and walked up the steps leading into building. Being cut off from her family stung now more than ever. If she had a difficult pregnancy or if her baby had health challenges, her parents were willing to let her handle things all by herself. She could hardly believe it. She'd never even set eyes on her son or daughter, and she couldn't imagine ever leaving them in this position. Totally and completely alone.

Except Finn was here, just as he'd promised. And he'd taken a vow to be by her side, no matter what happened.

The gravity of such a promise hit her hard as she checked in with the receptionist and filled out all the necessary medical forms. This was serious. There were pages and pages of questions to be answered and information to process. It all seemed to pass in a worrisome, overwhelming blur until at last she was wearing a paper gown and lying on an examination table beside an ultrasound machine.

After spending most of the morning in the waiting room, Finn now sat, stone-faced, in a chair facing the dark screen. Upon Avery's request, the nurse had gone to find him so they could both catch their first glimpse of the baby at the same time. There was still a layer of tension between them that hadn't been there before their night in the honeymoon suite at Maverick Manor. Although if she was truly being honest with herself, the strain in their relationship had raised its ugly head when she'd first told him about the pregnancy. It was just much more obvious since the tender moment they'd shared when he carried her over the threshold.

He was angry, and Avery could totally understand why. The secret had gotten away from her faster than she could figure out what to do with it, and now she was paying the price. Just because Finn was so eager to put a ring on her finger didn't mean he'd forgiven her.

Nor did it mean that he loved her.

Still, she was so glad to have him sitting there beside her that she could have cried.

"Okay, let's see what we have here." The doctor smiled at Avery and covered her belly with some type of gel.

Then she pressed a device that reminded Avery of a large computer mouse over her abdomen, and the screen lit up with moving shadows in various shades of gray.

The doctor confirmed what they both already knew—Avery's due date lined up perfectly with their night together in Oklahoma as the time of conception. But what Avery wanted most of all was a clear view of the baby, yet she couldn't make sense of the blurry images on the monitor.

And then all the breath in her body seemed to bottle up in her chest as a delicate profile came into view, followed by a glimpse of a tiny foot with five tiny, perfect toes.

"Are you two interested in having one of those trendy gender reveal parties? Or should I go ahead and spill the beans?" the doctor asked.

"Spill," Avery said. "Please."

There'd been enough surprises already. Besides, how could she have a gender reveal party when her own family wasn't even speaking to her?

"In that case, there she is," the doctor said, smiling.

Finn's gaze flew to meet Avery's, and all the things they couldn't seem to say to each other—all the hidden fears and insecurities, all the doubts, tempered by an aching, raw longing for connection—melted away.

There she is.

A little girl. Their daughter—hers and Finn's.

Chapter Twelve

Avery was relieved that seeing the sonogram alleviated some of the tension between her and Finn. A week later, they were still getting along well enough that the Crawfords seemed to genuinely believe they were in love. Even Melba and Old Gene had fallen for the ruse, showering them with congratulations and best wishes upon their return to Rust Creek Falls.

They'd moved into Finn's suite at the Ambling A, which so far had been spacious enough for them to move about in separate orbits. At night, Avery slept in Finn's king-size bed, with its rustic Aspen log frame and sheets that smelled of sandalwood, hay and warm leather. Of Finn.

Her husband camped out on the oversize leather sofa adjacent to the bed, far enough away to avoid any accidental physical contact, but close enough for Avery to grow accustomed to the rhythmic sound of his breathing in the dark. He hadn't touched her at all since she'd taken up residence in his home—not even a casual hug or innocent brush of his fingertips—and somehow hearing him sleep so close by made her feel a little less lonely. A little less like an outsider on Crawford territory.

They weren't going to get away with the lack of physical affection for long—not if everyone was going to remain convinced that they were actual, real newlyweds. But Avery was grateful for a little breathing room.

By the time she and Finn joined the rest of the Crawford clan at the annual Rust Creek Falls Halloween costume party, she'd foolishly begun to believe she had enough of a handle on her emotions to withstand a lengthy public charade.

She was wrong, of course.

So.

Very.

Wrong.

The party was held in the high school gym, which someone had spent a serious amount of effort transforming into a Halloween-themed delight. There was a maze made of hay bales off to the side, swags of twisted orange and black crepe paper and more fake spiderwebs than Avery had ever seen in one place before. As promised, Melba had made her famous caramel apples, and when Avery and Finn arrived, children dressed as ghosts, ballerinas and superheroes had clearly been enjoying the sweet treats, as evidenced by their sticky chins.

Avery couldn't help but smile. She'd never been to a party like this one before, not even when she was a child. She couldn't remember ever going trick-or-treating, either. Halloween night in Dallas always meant the mayor's posh Masquerade Ball, held at an exclusive hotel overlooking the city skyline. Invitations to the fancy masked ball were coveted, and Avery and her parents were always regulars. When she'd been a little girl, she'd stayed at home with the nanny and watched while her parents headed off to the party, dressed in opulent Halloween finery.

But this, she thought as she looked around the gym, *this is what a Halloween party should look like.*

She loved it all, from the happy children and homemade treats to the makeshift dance floor where an adult dressed as Frankenstein's monster was leading a group in a dance to the "Monster Mash."

"Wait a minute." Avery took a closer look at the face beneath the green makeup. "Is that your father out there on the dance floor?"

Finn shook his head and let out a wry laugh. "It certainly looks that way."

"Hey, it's about time the lovebirds arrived." Wilder, wrapped in bandages to look like a mummy, handed Finn a beer and gave Avery a peck on the cheek. "The gang's all here."

He wasn't kidding. The Crawfords were camped out at two adjoining picnic tables right in the center of the action. All five of Finn's brothers were there, accompanied, of course, by their respective wives and children—Logan and Sarah with baby Sophia, Xander and Lily, Knox and Genevieve, Hunter with Wren. Since Avery's surprise wedding to

Finn, Wilder and Hunter were the only two remaining single brothers, and neither had dates for the costume party—unless Hunter's daughter counted. Avery certainly thought so. They looked like the perfect father-daughter Halloween duo, with Wren dressed in a puffy tulle princess gown and Hunter wearing a large cardboard rectangle covered in tinfoil strapped to his chest.

"What are you supposed to be, dude?" Finn cast a dubious glance at Hunter's cardboard accessory. Its tinfoil covering was starting to look a little worse for wear. "A robot?"

Hunter's face fell. "No."

"He's a knight in shining armor," Avery said, winking at Wren. "Obviously. You and your daddy match, don't you?"

"Yes!" Wren giggled and pointed at the plastic crown perched atop her silky blond hair. "I'm a princess, and Daddy is a knight."

"I totally see it," Avery said, struggling to keep a straight face as Finn shook his head at Hunter.

"Nope. That—" he pointed at Hunter's sad silver shield "—is weak. Don't tell me you couldn't come up with a more convincing knight getup."

Hunter glowered at him.

Avery thought it was sweet that Hunter had gone to the effort to try to make a costume.

"Cut your brother some slack." Avery gave Finn a playful little shoulder bump and then froze when she realized what she'd done.

She'd initiated contact—a clear violation of their unspoken agreement not to touch one another, because as they both knew, one thing could very well lead to another. Before the marriage, they'd agreed to no sex. But since the wedding night, they hadn't so much as kissed. Somewhere along the way, the no-sex rule had snowballed into something else. It was as if they were both going out of their way to avoid any physical contact whatsoever.

Avery crossed her arms, uncrossed them and then crossed them again, painfully aware of every part of her body relative to Finn's. Less than inch of space existed between her arm and his chest, and the air in that space felt electric all of a sudden.

A shiver coursed through her while she tried to concentrate on what Hunter was saying.

"I'm doing the best I can." He rested a hand on top of Wren's slender shoulder and gave it a squeeze. "You'll understand one day when you have kids."

Finn practically choked on his beer.

"When's that going to be, anyway?" Wilder grinned at Finn. "You were in such a hurry to put a ring on this lady's finger, I figure you'll be wanting to start a family sooner rather than later."

Avery didn't dare look at Finn. If she did, the truth surely would be written all over her face.

"Give us time" was all he said in response, but when the conversation turned to other, less panic-inducing matters, he slipped his arm around her waist and pulled her close.

Little fires seemed to skitter over her skin everywhere he touched her. Her brain told her to pull away, to save herself. But her body had other ideas. Every cell in her body seemed to sigh with relief at once again being so near to the man she'd married...the man she was afraid she was starting to care for far more than she'd ever intended.

Their eyes met, and then his gaze flitted to her lips. He quickly looked away.

It's all just for show. She needed that reminder. They were newlyweds. His family was watching...the entire town was watching. They needed to make it look real. After all, that's why they'd come to the party dressed in matching bride and groom costumes.

She just wished it didn't *feel* so real.

She did her best to shift her attention elsewhere. Maximilian seemed to be hitting the dance floor with a different partner every time the song changed. His partners ranged from small children he let stand on his feet as he spun them around to women his own age, and everyone else in between. Avery couldn't help but laugh. For a man who seemed so invested in marrying off his sons, he sure was a flirt. The biggest one in Rust Creek Falls, so it seemed.

"Avery." Little Wren tugged on the sleeve of Avery's white dress to get her attention.

"Yes, sweetie?" Avery took a seat on the picnic bench so that they were eye to eye. Finn's fingertips slid casually to the back of her neck, where he toyed languidly with a lock of her hair.

It's only make-believe, no more real than Hunter's tinfoil shield.

"You and Uncle Finn just got married, right?" Wren smoothed down the front of her pink tulle gown. Hunter had chosen the DIY route for his own costume, but he'd obviously steered clear of Pinterest for his daughter's. She looked like a mini Disney princess, all the way down to the petite velvet slippers on her feet.

"We did." Avery nodded, pushing the cheap tulle veil on her head away from her eyes.

Wren's little brow furrowed. "Why didn't you have a fancy wedding with a big white dress?"

"Oh. Well." Avery's heart was in her throat all of a sudden, and her simple bride costume made her feel more like a fraud than ever before. "Not everyone has a fancy wedding. What matters most is finding someone you care about, someone you know you'll love." She swallowed. Hard. "Forever and ever."

"Like happily-ever-after?" Wren said.

Avery nodded, not quite trusting herself to speak.

"Life is perfect when you're a princess or a bride." The little girl spun in a circle with her hands clasped in front of her as if she were holding a bridal bouquet.

Perfect?

Not quite. Avery was a bride, and her life was far from perfect. Sometimes she wished she'd never thought to make her marriage to Finn a business arrangement. Would it really be so terrible to try to make things work? They were having a baby together, after all.

"I can't wait until I'm a bride one day," Wren said, running her tiny fingers over Avery's short costume wedding dress.

And then she skipped away, a vision

in tulle, and Avery couldn't help but feel like she'd just had a conversation with her younger self.

Had she really ever been as innocent and starry-eyed as Wren?

Yes, she had. And despite everything, a part of her—the wishful, hopeful part that seemed to rise from the ashes every time she looked at Finn—still was.

But she wasn't a child anymore. It had been years since she'd trusted in fairy-tale endings, and Finn had never tried to pretend he was her Prince Charming. He'd always been up front and honest about what they'd had. Not a lifetime, but a night. Just one…until the baby had come along. It was a shame little girls were set up with such high expectations.

Real life was so seldom as perfect as Wren believed.

Avery was gone.

One minute, she'd been chatting with

Wren, and the next time Finn glanced in her direction, she wasn't here.

He frowned into his beer as his brothers continued their running commentary of Maximilian's efforts to charm Melba Strickland onto the dance floor. It wasn't going well for Max. According to town lore, she'd never danced with a man other than Old Gene, and by all appearances, it was going to stay that way.

"Denied." Wilder let out a laugh. "Again."

Finn glanced toward the games area of the gym, where Wren, Lily, Genevieve and Sarah were participating in a race in which they wrapped each other in spools of white gauze to look like mummies. Still no Avery.

"You're missing it." Hunter gave Finn a nudge with his elbow. "I swear Melba is on the verge of conking Dad in the head with one of her caramel apples."

"What?" Finn said absently as he continued scanning the surroundings in search of his wife.

"Hey." Hunter nudged him harder. "What's with you?"

"I can't find Avery."

Hunter shrugged. "She was here a few minutes ago. She probably went to the bar for a beer."

Wrong on both counts. Avery wasn't drinking because of her pregnancy, and it had been longer than a mere few minutes since he'd seen her last.

"I'm going to go look for her." Finn shoved his beer at Hunter.

He took it and shrugged. "Suit yourself, but if you're just looking for an excuse to run off and take your wife to bed, you could have just said so."

Finn grunted a noncommittal response and went to weave his way through the crowd, but he couldn't find Avery anywhere. Panic coiled into a tight knot in the pit of his stomach.

What if something was wrong, either with her or the baby?

She would have said something to him if she wasn't feeling well, wouldn't she?

He didn't want to worry his family or the Stricklands, so instead of asking Melba or one of his female relatives to take a look in the ladies' room, he knocked on the door himself. Still no luck. She wasn't anywhere in the gymnasium.

Adrenaline shot through him, causing a terrible tingle in his chest. He needed to find her. Now.

Finn fled the party without saying goodbye. If he told the other Crawfords why he was so desperate to find Avery, he'd end up outing her pregnancy when he'd promised her they would wait to tell everyone. But if she wasn't in the parking lot or right outside the building, he was going to have to get help from someone. She hadn't just vanished into thin air.

He pushed through the double doors of the gym, squinting into the darkness. The moon hung low in the sky overhead, so big and round it looked swollen. A harvest moon spilling amber light over the horizon.

And in the distance he saw her— Avery, so beautiful in the moonlight— sitting on a playground swing, looking even more like a bride than she had on their wedding day.

Stone-cold relief washed over him. He was too happy to see her to let himself be irritated at her for disappearing like that. He rushed toward her, swallowing the pavement with big strides, but then someone cut into his path. A woman.

"This must be my lucky night," she said, gazing up at him from beneath the brim of a witch's hat.

Finn had no clue as to the woman's identity, other than the generic naughty-witch vibe she was giving off in her skimpy costume. Didn't she know this was an old-fashioned family-friendly party?

"Sorry, I'm on my way…" He gestured vaguely toward the swing set, where Avery lifted her head and met his gaze.

"You're Finn Crawford," the witch said. "At long last. I've been trying to get ahold of you for days."

"What?" He dragged his attention away from Avery to look at the woman again. "I'm sorry. I don't think we've met."

"We haven't, but Viv Dalton assured me you'd be interested in making my acquaintance. I'm Natalie." The witch batted her purple eyelashes at him and laid a hand on his chest.

He gently but firmly removed it. "I think there's been a misunderstanding."

This must be the woman who'd been blowing up his cell a few days ago, the same woman who'd called the Ambling A and spoken to Maximilian.

"I'm not dating anymore," he said. "I actually just got married."

"So that's not just a costume?" The witch blinked in the direction of his tuxedo T-shirt and his adhesive "groom" name tag. Her face fell. "Oh. Too bad."

"Again, sorry. But I really need to go." He looked past her toward the playground, but the swing set was empty now. One empty, lonely swing moved back and forth.

Damn it.

She was gone again.

"Avery?" He called out, jogging toward the playground. She couldn't have gone far. "Avery! Where are you?"

He found her clear around the corner, stomping down North Buckskin Road, her costume bridal veil whipping furiously around her head.

"Avery, thank God," he said, breathing hard as he struggled to catch up. "You had me worried sick."

She rolled her eyes and kept on walking, and it wasn't until she passed beneath a streetlamp that he noticed the dark rings of mascara under her eyes. His gut churned.

She'd been crying.

"Where are you going? What's wrong?"

"Back to the boarding house." She sniffed and kept marching toward Cedar Street, where the old purple Victorian loomed at the intersection.

The panicked knot in the pit of Finn's stomach tightened until he was almost gasping for air. "What? Why?"

"I miss Pumpkin, and I don't want to be anywhere near you right now." She stopped abruptly and glared at him. "I'd much prefer the company of a baby goat to you at the moment."

"Because of the witch?" He glanced over his shoulder toward the high school and then fixed his gaze with Avery's again. She was angry—clearly—but somewhere beneath the glittering fury in her big doe eyes, he saw something else. Hurt.

"Avery." He shook his head and jammed his hands on his hips to stop himself from reaching for her...from plunging his hands in her hair and kissing her full on the lips in flagrant violation of their marital agreement. "Princess, she's no one. Just some woman Viv Dalton wanted to set me up with a while back. But that was after I found out you were here, so obviously I told her no."

Avery glanced up at him for a second, then resumed staring at a spot somewhere to his left. Clearly, she had no interest in even looking at him.

"If you'd stuck around back there, you would have heard me tell Viv's witch that I'd just gotten married and that I couldn't stop for a chat because I'd come outside looking for *you*."

Avery narrowed her gaze at him and

squared her shoulders. "I wasn't jealous, if that's what you're thinking."

Liar.

Finn didn't dare laugh, but he was temped. "Is that so, wifey?"

"Okay, maybe I was just a little." She held her pointer finger and thumb a sliver apart. "An infinitesimal amount."

"Got it." He nodded, and the adrenaline flooding his body shifted into something else far more familiar, far more dangerous under the circumstances. Desire. "You're hightailing it back to the boarding house because you were jealous to see me talking to another woman."

He took a step closer, needing her softness. Her heat. "Even though you have no interest whatsoever in sleeping with me."

Her lips parted, and the tip of her cherry-red tongue darted out to wet them. Finn instantly went hard.

She lifted her chin, determined to stand her ground even though they both knew she'd just showed her hand. She wanted him just as badly as he wanted her. "I already told you why I was going back. I miss Pumpkin."

"So this wild-goose chase you've got me on is about a goat?" He wasn't buying it, not even for a second.

"Yes." She huffed out a sigh. "Mostly. Plus I was talking to Wren and she asked me why we didn't have a big wedding. She told me she couldn't wait to be a bride one day, just like me. And I just… I can't…"

Tears shimmered in her eyes, sparkling like diamonds in the moonlight. "What are we doing, Finn?"

He'd made Avery a promise when she'd agreed to marry him. She'd asked so little of him, and he'd been determined to keep his word, no matter how agonizing that promise turned out to be.

Did she have any idea how many times he'd nearly slipped up and reached for her? A thousand times a day, whether to simply hold her hand, spread his palms over her belly to feel the life growing inside her—the life they'd made together—or to touch her in all the ways he dreamed about every night when he slept alone on his sad leather sofa.

His gaze bored into her as though that's all it would take for her to understand. As if he only needed to look at her hard enough for her to know how badly he ached for her. Then…now…always.

She was his. She'd *been* his all along. Didn't she know that?

Screw it.

He couldn't do it anymore, and from what she was telling him, neither could she. It was time to forget their silly rules and be honest with each other for a change.

"This," he said, lifting his hand to cup her chin between his thumb and forefinger. "*This* is what we're doing."

Then he touched his lips to hers with a gentleness in stark opposition to the riot taking place inside him. He wouldn't force himself on her—not now, not ever—and he needed some sort of confirmation that this was okay. That this was what she wanted, even though she'd been doing her level best to pretend otherwise.

That confirmation came in the form of a breathy, kittenish sigh and Avery's hands sliding around his neck, her nails digging feverishly into his back. Then she kissed him so hard he saw stars.

There's my girl, he thought. *There's my princess.*

And then there were no more thoughts, no more rules and no more walls as he scooped his wife into his arms and carried her to his truck in plain view of anyone who cared to look. Finn didn't give a damn about appearances. It was time to take his wife to bed.

Chapter Thirteen

We shouldn't be doing this.

Those words kept spinning through Avery's consciousness as she and Finn fumbled their way up the stairs of the log mansion at the Ambling A, kissing and shedding articles of clothing along the way.

Thank goodness the rest of the family was still eating caramel apples and dancing to the "Monster Mash" back in the high school gymnasium. Because as desperately as she ached for her husband right now, she wasn't sure if she could have stopped for anyone or anything. Not even if Frankenstein's actual monster had been blocking their path to the bedroom.

We shouldn't be doing this.

Finn pressed her against the wall just outside his bedroom, and his lips moved away from her mouth, dragging slowly, deliciously down the side of her neck. She sagged against the cool pine, hands fisting in his hair as he kissed his way from one breast to the other.

They definitely shouldn't be doing *that*.

Stopping wasn't an option, though. It no longer mattered what they should or shouldn't be doing. Desire was moving through her with the force of a freight train, bearing down hard. She needed this. She'd needed this so badly for so long. It felt like forever since the last time Finn had touched her like this, the last time he'd laid her down on the smooth sheets of his bed in Oklahoma and thrust inside her for the very first time.

The only time.

How was that even possible? She was made for this…made for him. They fit together like two halves of the same whole, and after they'd parted on that strange, sad morning in Oklahoma City, she'd never quite felt whole again. All these months it was as if she'd been walking around with a huge piece of herself missing, just out of reach.

And then…

Then she'd realized she was pregnant, and she'd somehow convinced herself that was the reason she'd been feeling so out of sorts. She wasn't in love with Finn Crawford. She couldn't be. They barely knew one another. The only thing she'd known for absolute certain was that he was a Crawford and that her father would probably drop dead on the spot if he ever found out they'd been intimate.

These were the things she'd told herself as she'd put away her pencil skirts, packed her yoga mat and headed to Rust Creek Falls. Love had nothing to do with her messy state of emotional disarray. It all boiled down to science. She was walking around with a piece of Finn Crawford inside her, his DNA had gone and gotten itself all mixed up with hers, and now her body was confused. It was as simple as that. Three out of four biologists would totally agree with her.

Lies.

Lies, lies and more lies.

Had she really been so foolish as to believe that she could come to the Ambling A and not end up right here, with Finn slowly walking her backward until her knees hit the edge of the bed and they tumbled together, already losing track of where her body ended and his began? Had she honestly thought she could marry him and keep up the whole virgin-bride routine in an effort to spare her heart?

It seemed ludicrous now. Why should she forgo *this*? Finn was her husband, and she was his wife. There was nothing whatsoever wrong with the way he gently parted her thighs and kissed his way down her body, his tongue warm and wicked against the cool of her skin. On the contrary, it was exquisite. She was lost in the moment in a way that she'd never managed to achieve, no matter how many hot yoga classes she'd attended or how often she'd used the meditation app on her phone.

No one existed outside her and Finn. There was no embarrassment, no worry as her hips moved up and down, undulating in perfect rhythm with the stroke of his fingers, searching…seeking the release that only he could give her. She was free and open in a way that she'd never been able to be with anyone else.

Because they were special. She could run all she wanted, but she'd always come back to this—to his hands sliding into her hair as his gaze burned into hers, branding her, soul-deep. To the flawless heat of his body perfectly poised over hers and the way he shuddered when he finally slid inside her. To the way she shattered around him instantly, crying out his name.

Finn.

It had always been him, and it always would be. Giving herself to him again changed nothing, because he'd captured her heart a long time ago.

Yet at the same time, it changed everything. Because somewhere beneath the honeyed heat of her desire, she remembered he'd never said it. The one thing she wanted to hear more than anything else in the world. *I love you.*

Her heart ached to hear it, but she managed to push her hunger for it down.

Deep down to the place where it had been since the moment Finn slipped the ring on her finger and she realized she wanted it to be real. For *them* to be real.

And she actually thought it would stay there. She believed she could spend her nights in Finn's bed, touching him, loving him, pretending he felt it even though he never said the words. Because sometimes pretending was better than nothing. Sometimes pretending was as good as it got.

But after it was over—after he'd stroked her to climax again and again, after he'd groaned her name and shuddered his release and they lay beside each other with legs and hearts intertwined—he did something that finally broke the pretense beyond repair.

He leaned over and, with the softest brush of his lips imaginable, he kissed her growing belly. And with an ache in his voice that she'd never heard before, he whispered a word. Just one. The most profoundly beautiful one he could have said.

Mine.

If only she could have made herself believe he'd been talking about her. Or them—her and the baby both. But he hadn't. He'd meant the child, their child, and while it was sweet, it just wasn't enough. And it never would be, because sometimes pretending was better than nothing, but when it wasn't, it was the most devastating heartbreak of all.

I can't stay here anymore.

The thought started as a spark, and in the hours before the sun came up, it exploded into a wildfire, burning out of control and destroying everything in its path—every last hope for a future, charred beyond recognition. She'd repeated it to herself so many times in the night that it became a balm, a way to calm the panic that threatened to eat her alive at the thought of saying goodbye. By the time Finn opened his eyes, she was already dressed, packed and ready to go. All she had to do was tell him.

"I can't stay here anymore."

Finn was dreaming.

No, it wasn't a dream. It was a nightmare—the worst nightmare his unconscious possibly could have conjured.

He closed his eyes and willed the image of Avery, fully clothed with one of her slick designer suitcases in her hand, out of his head. His mind was playing tricks on him. That had to be it. Last night had changed everything. He and Avery had finally stopped pretending and been honest with each other about their feelings. They'd made love.

And that's exactly what it had been, too. Not just sex. Things between him and Avery had never been just physical. He knew that now. On some level, he always had.

But no matter how hard he tried to keep his eyes closed and go back to the world from just hours before—the world where he and his wife were tangled in bedsheets—he couldn't. The space beside him was cold. Empty...

As empty as his heart felt when he opened his eyes and realized the sight in front of him wasn't a dream, after all. It was real.

"Excuse me?" he said, staring hard at Avery's suitcase.

When the hell had she packed it? Had she climbed out of his bed the moment he'd fallen asleep?

"I can't stay here," she repeated, a gut-wrenching echo.

He sat up, and the sheet fell away, exposing him. Avery took a sharp inhale and averted her gaze.

Seriously?

"Look at me, damn it," he growled.

"What are talking about? You can't leave, Princess. You just…"

…can't.

What would he say to his family when they woke up and found out she'd left? What would he do? They were a family. She couldn't just leave.

But apparently she could, because she was already walking toward the door.

Out of his bed.

Out of his life.

"No." Finn jumped up and went after her. "Whatever's wrong, we can fix it. Let me fix it, Princess. Please."

He'd never allowed himself to be more vulnerable in his life. He was naked and begging, but he didn't care.

"We can take things slow, if that's what you want," he blurted as her hand gripped the doorknob.

She paused, just long enough to shake her head.

"Finn, we…"

"What happened last night doesn't have to happen again. We can wait. We can do whatever you want. Just don't leave."

"Can't you see?" She shook her head again. "I have to. I just need some space. Please."

Space.

He could give her that, couldn't he? Maybe a night or two at the boarding house would do them both some good.

No. Finn glared at her. He wanted her here, with him. He needed his wife and his baby. He needed them as surely as he needed his next breath.

"You're my wife. We had a deal, re-member?" he said. Married…till death do them part.

God, what was wrong with him? He sounded as controlling and manipulative as his father.

"You're right." Avery looked past him, toward the bed. "And last night we broke that deal. So now all bets are off."

"Avery." He raked a hand through his hair, tugging hard at the ends. "I'm..."

He couldn't bring himself to say he was sorry. Because he wasn't. Not entirely. What had happened between them last night had been honest and real. Even more authentic than the band of gold around Avery's finger. She knew it as well as he did. Why else would she be running scared?

But even as he prepared to stand his ground stubbornly, he realized that somewhere deep down, he *was*. He was sorry for anything that made Avery hurt or made her afraid. Because all he wanted was to make her feel loved. And safe in his arms.

He took a deep breath and forced the words out. "I'm sorry."

It didn't matter. Nothing he said mattered, because she'd already made up her mind.

"Me, too," she said quietly.

And then she walked right out the door, taking Finn's baby and every battered beat of his heart with her as she left.

Avery's nonstop flight to Dallas felt like the longest two and a half hours of her life.

She did everything she could to make the time pass as quickly as possible, from her stack of glossy fashion magazines to the vast array of snacks she'd picked up at the airport gift shop. But living at the boarding house for so long had changed Avery's eating habits. She much preferred Melba's and Claire's home cooking to the quick grab-and-go fare and Lean Cuisines she'd lived on while she'd been so busy helping run Ellington Meats. And as it turned out, she'd even lost all enthusiasm for her beloved *Vogue*, *Elle* and *Harper's Bazaar* now that she could no longer wear any of the sleek, fitted clothes featured on their pages.

Or maybe she'd simply developed a sudden fondness for flannel and cowboy boots.

Good grief, what was happening to her? Tastes changed, she supposed. The delicate rose gold ring on her finger was perhaps the most glaringly obvious testament to that fact, from the ring itself to the marriage it represented. Her father would probably have a heart attack the minute he saw it.

She thought about removing the ring before the plane landed, but she just couldn't bring herself to do so. She'd told Finn she was leaving, but she hadn't said a word about ending their marriage. That was a given, though, wasn't it? Part of the condition of coming home had always been cutting Finn out of her life. As welcoming as her parents had been on the phone when she'd broken down and called them from the airport in Montana, she had no reason to believe that had changed.

Taking the ring off seemed so final, though. The ultimate ending to a book she wasn't sure she was capable of closing. She just knew she needed time away from Rust Creek Falls to clear her head and figure out what was truly best for her and her baby. But if sleeping with Finn had confirmed anything, it was that she wasn't built for a marriage of convenience. She'd been fooling herself thinking she could marry a man and not become emotionally attached, especially a man she was already head over heels in love with.

When her flight finally landed in Dallas, she deplaned with nothing but a lump in her throat and her lone carry-on bag. It seemed impossible that she would come home with so little physical evidence of a life-changing month away. Her time in

Montana almost felt like a fever dream, too colorful and lush to be real. But that was the whole point, wasn't it? None of it had been real. And now here she was, back on Texas soil with her smallest Louis Vuitton rolling bag and more emotional baggage than she could possibly carry all on her own.

When she saw her mother and father waiting for her just outside the security gate, she braced herself for a flood of emotions. But when her mother gathered her into her arms, Avery didn't even cry. Not a single, solitary tear. She'd come crawling home with her tail between her legs, but at the very least she'd expected to feel a small sense of relief.

After all, she was back in the fold. Her heart was safe now.

Then why did she feel nothing but a horrible numbness and the nagging sense that she'd just made the biggest mistake of her life?

* * *

It was a short ride from the airport to the Ellington family home in the moneyed neighborhood of Highland Park, and Avery's parents spent it getting her caught up on everything she'd missed while she'd been away.

Her mother told her about the latest happenings at the country club in lurid detail and suggested now that Avery was back, she might want to help cochair the upcoming Junior League charity fundraiser. The lawn of the big gothic church on University Drive was a sea of orange now that the annual pumpkin patch was in full swing, and the mayor was throwing his annual Masquerade Ball. Avery had come just in time.

But the Masquerade Ball wouldn't be anything like the sweet Halloween dance she'd attended with the Crawfords. There wouldn't be any costumed children or fake spiderwebs or bobbing for apples. It would be a staid affair, perfectly planned, perfectly decorated and perfectly boring. She missed the small-town charm of Rust Creek Falls already.

Meanwhile, her father filled her in on what she'd missed at the office. He'd promoted one of the project managers in her absence, but her corner office was still ready and waiting for her. She could walk back into her old life just like nothing had ever happened. It would be as if she'd never gone to Rust Creek Falls at all.

Except she had.

She stared blankly ahead as the big iron gate at the foot of the driveway swung open and her father's Cadillac Escalade cruised past the security cameras. Neither of her parents had mentioned her pregnancy. Were they just going to pretend that she wasn't having Finn Crawford's baby in a few months' time? Was that how this strange homecoming was going to play out?

Her hand went instinctively to her baby bump, and a tiny nudge pressed against her palm, just as it had when she'd exchanged vows with Finn in the country courthouse in Great Gulch. Finally, something real she could grasp hold of. Her child. Avery was going to be a mother, and no amount of pretending could prove otherwise.

"I'm married," she said quietly as her father shifted the car into Park.

"Oh, dear." Her mother sighed. Finally she had something more pressing to worry about than the centerpieces for the next country club luncheon.

Her father's gaze locked with hers in the reflection of the rearview mirror. "I saw the ring and figured as much."

She bit her lip and nodded. Good. Perhaps their bizarre sense of denial wasn't as serious as she'd begun to think.

"That's what annulments are for. Our attorney can get this taken care of in a matter of days." Her dad shrugged one shoulder and then got out of the car and shut the door as if the matter had been settled once and for all.

All of Avery's breath bottled up in her throat. An annulment. Could she do that Finn? Did she even want to?

"Honey," her mom said, turning to rest a hand on Avery's knee. "Give your daddy time. We can talk about all of this later. The most important thing is that you're home now."

Avery nodded as she blinked back tears. Only they weren't the tears of relief she'd expected. They were something else, something too horrible and painful to name.

She climbed out of the car and went straight to her childhood bedroom at the top of the home's curved staircase. She passed the grand piano where she'd taken lessons as a little girl and the framed collection of photographs that lined the hallway—Avery as homecoming queen of her private high school, Avery dressed in a white satin gown and elegant elbow-length gloves at her debutante ball, her father spinning her across the dance floor at the father-daughter dance.

It didn't matter how old she was, how well she did at the office or even if she was pregnant, her father would always see her just like those framed images—as his daughter. Just a little girl, barely more than an extension of himself.

How had she never noticed this before? Sure, she'd always been a daddy's girl, following in her father's footsteps and working alongside him at the family business. Daddy's princess. But she'd always thought it had been her choice. *Her* path.

Had it? Had she ever been the one in charge of her own life?

It was all so confusing, and two hours later, once she'd showered, changed and gone back downstairs for dinner, she wasn't any closer to knowing the answer to the many questions spinning around in her head. She was only certain of one thing—the decision whether or not to end her marriage was hers and hers alone.

"Are you feeling better now, dear?" Avery's mom cast a surprised glance at the buffalo-checkered shirt she'd slipped into—one of her purchases from the general store—but refrained from asking why she hadn't dressed for dinner. Mealtime in the Ellington household had always been a rather formal affair.

"A little. I'm really tired." Avery took her seat, the same place she'd sat for every family meal of her life.

As usual, her father was already seated at the head of the table. "You'll feel back to your old self once you get some rest.

Leave all the legal details to me. I'll meet with the lawyers first thing tomorrow and get the ball rolling."

Avery picked up her fork but set it back down. "Daddy, no. I'm not ready."

Oscar glanced at his wife, cleared his throat and then spread his napkin carefully in his lap. "Very well. We can discuss the legalities later."

"Absolutely." Her mother beamed. "Avery, I was thinking we could start decorating the bedroom next door to yours for the baby. Won't that be fun?"

Avery blinked. "What about my place?"

She hadn't protested when they'd taken her straight to the big Ellington mansion from the airport, but surely they didn't expect her to *live* here from now on. She was an adult, with her own townhome near the Galleria.

"We can get a crib for there, too, if you like. But you're going to need help when the baby comes. We just assumed you'd want to stay here for a while." Her mother passed her a bowl of green beans.

Avery scooped some onto her plate and passed it to her father.

"We're just so glad you've finally come to your senses," he said. "Your child will have everything her little heart desires. She'll want for nothing."

Finally, they were talking about the baby. They were saying all the right things, making plans and acting like doting grandparents. Avery's childhood had been a happy one, and if her daughter grew up with the same upbringing, she'd no doubt be a happy, charmed little girl.

She'll want for nothing.

The words echoed in Avery's mind on repeat.

Right, she thought. *But what about what I want?*

Chapter Fourteen

Finn parked his rental car at the curb in front of the Georgian-style columned mansion on one of Highland Park's most prestigious streets. The driveway was blocked by a black steel gate with scrolled trim and a crest featuring a single cursive letter. *E* for Ellington.

Was he really going to just walk up to the front door and ring the bell of Oscar Ellington's home when he knew good and well he wasn't welcome here? Hell yes, he was.

Avery had *left* him. And she hadn't simply moved back down the road to Strickland's Boarding House. She'd gone all the way back to Texas, and she hadn't even bothered to give him the news herself. Melba and Old Gene had broken it to him when he'd shown up, desperate to talk to Avery. Melba had even gotten a little teary-eyed. She sat Finn down and tried to feed him some fresh caramel snickerdoodle cookies she'd just made for her boarders, but he couldn't eat. If Avery had gone back to Dallas, it meant only one thing—she'd agreed to her father's ridiculous terms.

Finn hadn't just lost his wife.

He'd lost his daughter, too.

He climbed out of the car and slammed the door. If Avery thought he was going to let her go straight from his bed back to her father without trying to talk some sense into her, she was dead wrong. He had a good idea what this was all about, anyway. They'd broken her sacred no-sex rule. Their fake marriage had suddenly become far too real, and she was running scared.

It would be okay, though. *They* would be okay. They had to be, because if Finn had learned anything in the days since he'd exchanged vows with Avery, it was that he couldn't live without her. Their fake marriage had always been real to him.

He simply needed to talk to her and assure her they could take things as slowly as she needed to. He'd do whatever she wanted, save for one thing—he'd never, ever let her family keep him from seeing his child.

Every damn flight from Montana to Dallas had been booked solid. Avery must have gotten the lone remaining seat on one of the last flights out. Thank God he'd remembered Maximilian's offer to send them off on a private jet for their honeymoon. When Finn told his father why he needed it, he hadn't even hesitated. The plane had been all fueled up, ready and waiting when Finn got to the airport in Billings.

His first stop upon landing had been Avery's town house, but her doorman assured Finn she'd been gone for weeks. There was only one place else she could be—the stately redbrick home in front of him. He gritted his teeth, pressed the doorbell and hoped against hope Avery would come to the door.

No such luck. *No one* came to the door. Instead, an older man's voice boomed through a small speaker situated next to the bell. "Sorry, son. This isn't a good time."

Finn's blood boiled at the sound of Oscar Ellington's condescending tone. He glanced around, trying to figure out how he'd already been identified. Sure enough, there were security cameras stationed in four different corners of the mansion's veranda.

He stared the closest one down. "I've come all the way from Montana. The least you can do is open the door."

"We're in the middle of dinner. Like I said, it's not a good time."

Seriously? He wasn't even going to come to the door?

Finn didn't know why he was surprised. The man had disowned his own daughter—his *pregnant* daughter, who'd always been daddy's little princess until she'd started calling the shots in her own life. Why would he suddenly be reasonable just because Finn had been on a wild-goose chase across the country?

He rang the bell again. Once, twice, three times.

"Am I going to have to call the police?" Oscar bellowed over the intercom.

If he wanted a screaming match, Finn was more than game. He yelled at the intercom, "Call whoever you want. I've come to take my wife home, and I'm not leaving here without her."

Across the street, a security guard's car rolled to a stop. Maybe Oscar wouldn't need to call the cops. It looked as though the neighborhood watch had that covered.

He beat on the door with a fist. He was done wasting time with the stupid bell and the prissy little intercom. Oscar needed to come outside so they could discuss the situation like men.

But the next voice to come over the intercom wasn't Oscar's. It was Avery's.

"Finn? Is that you?"

He nearly wept with relief at the sound of her soft Texas twang. Less than twelve hours ago, she'd been naked in his bed, and now they were talking through a speaker.

He fixed his gaze on the closest security camera. "Avery, baby. It's me. I've come to take you home. Whatever is wrong, we can fix it. Please, you've got to let me fix it."

"Can't you see that she's made her choice? My daughter wants nothing to do with you. For the last time, I'm ordering you to vacate the premises." Oscar's tone wasn't any more sympathetic than it had been before Avery joined the discussion, and somehow Finn doubted what he was saying was true.

Avery was running scared, but had she really told her father she wanted nothing more to do with him? He didn't want to believe it, but despair had begun to tie itself in knots in the pit of his stomach. He needed to see his wife. He needed to look her in the eye and tell her everything would be all right if she would just come home.

Every muscle in his body tensed. If Oscar didn't open the door, Finn was going to tear it down with his bare hands.

"Daddy, stop," Avery pleaded.

She was crying again, damn it. What was her father thinking? She was pregnant. If he hurt her...if he hurt the baby...

Heat flushed through Finn's body. He felt like he was on the verge of some kind of breakdown, breathing in ragged gulps until he felt like he was choking.

And then, by some miracle, the door swung open.

His head jerked up. He wasn't sure whether to expect Avery or her father as hope and dread danced a terrible duet in his consciousness.

But it was neither of them. Instead, an older woman with Avery's kind eyes stood on the threshold. "You must be Finn. I'm Avery's mother, Marion."

"Hello, ma'am." Finn tipped his hat. "I'm sorry for the...ah...disruption. But—"

She held up her hands. "Don't apologize. I understand this is a volatile situation, and I want to invite you in so we can all discuss this like reasonable adults."

He nodded, wanting to trust her but fully expecting Oscar to appear out of nowhere and slam the door in his face.

"Please, Finn." She held the door open wide, and for better or for worse, he stepped inside.

Avery had never thought she'd see the day Finn Crawford would be standing inside the house where she'd grown up, but here he was…in the flesh. And much to her irritation, that flesh looked even better than she remembered it. Was it possible that her husband had gotten even more handsome in the twelve hours or so since she'd last seen him?

It wasn't, right? Which meant the reason the sight of him sent shivers through every nerve ending of her body was because she'd missed him. She'd missed him more than she could fathom, but that didn't mean she was going to simply stand by and let the two men in her life argue over her as if she was one of their cattle.

At the moment, Finn and Oscar were staring daggers at each other with nothing but her mother's antique Chippendale coffee table between them to prevent an epic physical altercation. It was beyond ridiculous, and Avery was over it.

"Have you two completely lost your minds?" she spat.

They both started blaming each other at once, her father bellowing on about Maximilian, and Finn insisting that Avery pack her bags immediately and head back to the Ambling A. The crystal chandelier hanging overhead nearly shook from all the yelling.

Avery clamped her hands over her ears as tears streamed down her face. How was she supposed to make sense of anything when they were behaving this way? Maybe she should forget about Montana and Texas altogether and go raise her child on a desert island somewhere.

"Everyone, just settle down," her mother said calmly. "Or *I'll* call the police on *both* of you."

Oscar reared back as if someone had slapped him. Avery probably did as well, seeing as she'd never heard her mother speak to him like that before. Finn cast cautious glances all around.

Marion crossed her arms and continued, "Now that I have everyone's attention, why don't we all sit down? I told Finn we were going to have an adult conversation, and that's exactly what we're going to do."

No one moved a muscle. Finn and Oscar seemed to be engaged in some kind of alpha male contest to see who would comply first.

"That's it." Avery threw up her hands. "I've had enough of both of you."

Finn plopped down on the closest armchair so quickly it looked he was playing a game of musical chairs.

"I'm sitting. I'm ready." He fixed his gaze on her father. "Let's discuss this, Oscar. Man to man."

Her father sat, but not without commentary. "Fine, although there's not much to discuss. Avery left you to come home. I think that says it all."

Finn glanced at Avery, and the pain in his face was visceral. "With all due respect, sir. I'm Avery's husband, and her home is with me."

They were getting nowhere. Avery didn't know whether to cry or knock both their heads together.

"Enough," her mother said sharply. "This isn't for the two of you to decide. It's between Finn and Avery, no one else."

A tiny spark of hope ignited deep in Avery's soul. Finally, someone had said it. Whatever she and Finn felt—or didn't feel—for each other should be between them. She should have never agreed to marry him until the family drama had been sorted out, but she had.

She'd exchanged vows with Finn, all the while thinking she could protect herself from the feelings that came from a genuine relationship. So long as there was a wall between them, she'd be safe. In the end, though, it hadn't mattered how many bricks she stacked—she fell in love, anyway.

She *loved* Finn. Whether or not he loved her back no longer mattered. Her heart belonged to Finn Crawford, whether he wanted it or not.

Her mother's gaze shifted from Avery to Finn and back again. "You are having a baby together. This baby will bond you together for life."

The vows from their simple country wedding ceremony echoed in her mind, beating in time with her heart.

Until death do you part.

Marion's eyes narrowed, and for a moment, Avery felt as if her mother could see straight into her soul. "I think I know how each of you really feels about the other, but this is not for me to decide. You two need to figure it out…together."

She was right. Of course she was, but they still hadn't tackled the biggest elephant in the room—the angry bull elephant more commonly known as Oscar Ellington.

"As for you." Marion squared her shoulders and turned to face her husband. "I've stood for your nonsense long enough. You had no business cutting Avery off like you did. She's our daughter, our own flesh and blood, and you've been holding on to some silly grudge against Maximilian Crawford for far too long."

Oscar's face went three shades of red. Maybe four. It reminded Avery of the bright leaves back in the maple forest near Rust Creek Falls.

He seemed to know better than to interrupt, though. Marion Ellington rarely criticized her husband. Almost never, as far as Avery could remember. But her patience had finally cracked, and she was apparently finished holding her tongue.

"Either you give Avery back her inheritance—and her job—or I will leave you, Oscar Ellington. This is no idle threat. I will walk right out that door." She pointed to the front door with a trembling hand.

All eyes in the room swiveled toward Oscar. Avery didn't dare breathe while she waited for him to respond.

The silence stretched on for a long, loaded moment until he finally nodded. "As you wish."

Oscar's voice was quiet. Contrite.

When he turned a tender gaze toward Avery, her heart gave a tight squeeze. But what she nearly mistook for heartbreak was something else entirely—it was her heart, and her family, mending back into one unified piece after weeks of shattered silence.

"Your mother is right, sweetheart. I love you no matter what. If you want to stay married to a Crawford, I might not like it, but I'll learn to live with it." With a deep exhale, Oscar faced Finn full-on. "You obviously feel passionately about my daughter. I love her with my whole heart, and if you do, too, then I suppose it's possible for us to find some common ground."

A surreal feeling of euphoria washed over Avery. It started in her chest and spread outward, leaving a tingling surge in its wake.

Her father had just said everything Avery had wanted to hear from the moment she'd first realized she was pregnant. Before she'd even set foot in Rust Creek Falls, she'd lain awake nights, wishing and hoping for something like this to happen. It just seemed so impossible, and once he'd called her with the devastating news that he was cutting her off, she'd given up every last shred of hope.

Thank God for her mother.

If she hadn't intervened, they might never have gotten here. But she had, because that's what mothers did. They sacrificed all for their children. Avery was only beginning to understand the depth of that kind of unconditional love.

She rested her hand on her belly and fixed her gaze on Finn's. The feud was over. There was no longer anything standing between them. At long last, they could be together—*really* together—without the devastating heartbreak of being cut off from her family.

But now that all the obstacles had finally been torn down, Avery was no longer sure where she and Finn stood. A part of her—a very large, very real part—wanted to cross the room and throw herself at him the same way she had in the pasture at the Ambling A and in the cool quiet of the sugar bush at the syrup farm. Why shouldn't she? What her father thought no longer mattered.

But she'd left.

She'd finally given herself to Finn, and in the heady romance of the afterglow, she'd run away.

They could get past that, though, couldn't they? Everything had turned out for the best. Finn had followed her all the way here. And yet...

Finn was still sitting quietly on the rose damask sofa in the room where her mother threw tea parties. He hadn't uttered a word in response to what her father had just said.

I love her with my whole heart, and if you do, too, then I suppose it's possible for us to find some common ground.

This was the moment where Finn was supposed to confess his feelings. It was the only way to respond to that sort of statement, wasn't it?

I love Avery, too.

That's what Finn should be saying right now. Why wasn't he?

Please. Avery implored him with her gaze. Her feelings had to be written all over her face. Couldn't he see it? *Please, please say it.*

But suddenly Finn couldn't seem to look at her. The passion and fury that had driven him to fly all the way to Texas and practically beat down the door to the Ellington estate seemed to drain right out of him before her eyes.

He frowned down at his hands, folded neatly in his lap. Those hands had touched her in ways no one else ever had before. Those hands knew every inch of her body—every secret place, every soft, silken vulnerability. Avery couldn't look at them anymore without craving the exquisite pleasure of his skin against hers.

When Finn finally spoke, it was in a voice she'd never heard him use before. Quiet. Calm…terrifyingly so. "Can I have a word alone with Avery, please?"

"Of course," her mother said, rising to her feet as she shot a meaningful look at Oscar.

"Yes, yes." He stood as well, pausing to give Avery a kiss on the top of her head before they left the room. "I love you, honey. Remember that, okay? You have our support." He lingered for a moment, shifting awkwardly from foot to foot. "Whatever you decide."

It was strange seeing her father so unsure of himself and only underscored the gravity of what had just occurred. And what might happen next.

"I know." Avery reached out and squeezed his hand. "Thank you."

Finn's expression betrayed little as her parents left the room and closed the French doors, shutting them alone together inside. Avery no longer cared what exact words he uttered; she just wished he would say *something*. Anything.

"I—" She started to apologize for her disappearing act, but at the same exact time, Finn began talking, too.

"Avery—"

They both stopped abruptly and stared at each other. Another day, another time, they probably would have laughed. Neither one of them did so now, though. Avery's chin went wobbly like it always did when she was trying not to cry.

"This changes things," Finn finally said.

She blinked. "What does?"

"This." Finn gestured vaguely at their

surroundings—the antique rotary tele-
phone, the gilded wall mirror that had
been passed down from generation to
generation of Ellingtons, the grandfather clock with its familiar tick-tock
that Avery would have recognized blind-
folded.

The room they were sitting in hadn't
changed a bit since Avery's childhood.
She could have drawn a picture of it from
memory and not missed a single detail.

"You're back in the fold," he said. There
wasn't a drop of bitterness in his tone,
and Avery was suddenly unsure whether
that was a good sign or a bad one.

"I guess I am." She nodded. "But
shouldn't that be a good thing? My father is finally letting go of whatever happened between him and Maximilian. He
won't stop you from seeing the baby anymore."

"And you're no longer disinherited," he

added with a sad smile. "Which means you no longer need me."

Wait, that wasn't what it meant at all. Was that why he was acting so strangely all of a sudden? He thought the only reason they were together was because she'd had no place else to go?

Isn't it, though?

No.

She tried to swallow, but her throat had gone bone dry. It wasn't the only reason—not anymore. Deep down, it had never been the only reason. Finn was the father of her baby, but it was more than that, too. She'd *wanted* to exchange vows with him in that dusty old courthouse. She'd just been too afraid to admit it because Finn had never been the marrying type.

Oh, no.

Avery's heart plummeted to the soles of her feet. That's what the sudden change in Finn's mood was all about. He didn't want to be married. He never had. He'd just proposed because of the baby and now that there was no feud standing between him and his child, he was trying to let her down gently.

"You don't need me to support you and the baby," he said, spelling things out in a way that hurt more than she ever thought possible. As if all along she'd only been interested in the Crawford money.

"That's not true." She shook her head.

Stop it, she wanted to say. *Just stop saying these things and tell me you love me.*

"I think you need some time alone to figure out what it is you want, sweetheart." The kindness in his voice almost killed her. She'd rather he yell and scream than look at her the way he was looking at her right then…with goodbyes in his eyes.

Sure enough, he unfolded himself from the chair he was sitting in and loomed over her. Just as Avery expected, he already had one foot out the door.

She stood on wobbly legs and forced herself to meet his gaze. Where was the man who'd pounded on the front door with his fists, insisting he wasn't going anywhere without his wife by his side? She needed that man, whether he realized it or not. She *loved* that man.

"You know where to find me when you make up your mind."

They were the last words her husband said to her, followed by a chaste kiss on the cheek and a walk through the foyer to the front door.

And just like that, he was gone.

Chapter Fifteen

Avery couldn't seem to make herself move as the door shut softly yet firmly behind Finn. She wanted to go running after him. She wanted that more than anything in the world, but it was as if a physical force was holding her back, keeping her rooted to the spot.

He'd come all the way to Texas from Montana—for her. When she'd first spotted him on the security camera, she'd nearly wept with relief. If he'd chased her all the way to Texas, that had to mean he loved her.

Right?

She'd seen enough rom-coms to know that at some point, every good love story culminated in a grand romantic gesture. This was it. Finn had followed her to enemy territory so he could win her back.

But now that her mother had finally talked some sense into her father, Finn just up and walked away. There'd been no declaration of love, no promise of a future together. He'd spoken about their marriage as if it was precisely what she'd set out for it to be.

A business transaction.

And then he'd left her alone to think things through. God, it was humiliating. Avery didn't need to think, and she sure as heck didn't feel like being alone. She wanted Finn, damn it. Couldn't he see that? She was in love with him. She'd been in love with him all along, which was precisely why she'd been acting so crazy—kissing him one minute and running away the next. Even marrying him when they hardly knew each other.

Her behavior had nothing to do with pregnancy hormones. She was head over heels, crazy in love with her husband.

And he'd just walked right out the door.

She'd never felt so alone in her life, not even when her father had so coldly informed her that she'd been disinherited. She pressed a hand to her baby bump, desperate for a reminder that she wasn't completely on her own. She still had her daughter, and she always would.

And she could still have Finn, too. He'd made it perfectly clear that the decision was up to her. But was there really a decision to make if he didn't love her? How could she have been stupid enough to believe that exchanging sacred vows could ever be anything remotely similar to a business deal?

"Avery?" Her mom walked tentatively into the entryway and looked around. "Where's Finn?"

"He's…" *He's gone.* Avery shook her head. She couldn't say it. If she did, she'd break and she wasn't sure she'd ever be whole again.

"Oh, honey." Her mom wrapped her arms around Avery and hugged her tight. "Don't cry. Everything is going to be okay."

But it wasn't. There'd been no grand gesture, just a quiet goodbye, and now great heaving sobs were racking Avery's body. It was as if she'd been suppressing her real feelings for so long—since that fateful night in Oklahoma City—that she simply couldn't do it any longer. She was feeling everything at once. Joy and pain. Hope and fear. Love and loss.

So much loss that it nearly dragged her to her knees.

Her mother smoothed her hair back from her eyes, then cupped Avery's face in her hands. "Do you love him, sweetheart?"

She nodded as tears kept streaming down her face.

Her mom smiled as if she'd known as much all along. "Then it seems as though you have an important decision to make. Don't worry about your father. I'll handle him. You just do what you need to do."

Avery trembled all over.

Do what you need to do.

She took a ragged inhale as a terrible realization dawned—what she wanted to do and what she needed to do were two entirely different things.

The log mansion at the Ambling A was as quiet as a tomb when Finn walked through the door at three in the morning.

He was immensely grateful for Maximilian's access to a private plane, just as he'd been the day before when he was in such a hurry to get to Dallas.

But at the moment, he was even more grateful for the fact that all of his family members were in bed and he wouldn't have to see their disappointed expressions when he walked back through the door without his wife. The only thing that might have made him feel worse was the more likely possibility that they wouldn't have been surprised at all, that they'd have chalked up his short-lived marriage to Finn just being Finn. He never could commit to anyone or anything. Why should Avery be any different?

But she *was* different, damn it. She'd always been special. She was the one. She always had been, right from the start.

The baby mattered, obviously. Finn would lay down his life for his child, but

Avery mattered just as much. He'd only fully realized how much she meant to him after she'd left him. And now...

Now it was too late. She was back in Dallas, back in the loving arms of her family. Finn had his own opinions about what sort of father would ever turn his back on his pregnant adult daughter, but at least Oscar Ellington had done the right thing in the end.

If anyone understood the importance of family, it was Finn. As maddening as Maximilian could be, he'd been the one to raise six boys all on his own after his wife had walked out and left him. There was no denying Finn's father was a difficult man, and there was plenty of blame on both sides where his parents' divorce was concerned, but Maximilian had always been there for his sons. Always would be. Which was why Finn had tolerated his meddling into his sons' love lives as best as he could.

It was also why he'd done an about-face and hadn't insisted Avery return to the Ambling A with him. He couldn't make that choice for her. The last thing he wanted was to come between her and her family yet again. If they had any hope of remaining together, she'd have to make that decision on her own. He didn't want to be the kind of husband and father she'd grown up with. As much as he loved Avery, as much as he wanted her, he refused to bully her back into his home...into his life.

In a way, he'd already strong-armed her into marrying him. Witnessing the effect Oscar's controlling behavior had on the people he loved most in the world had been a wake-up call. Finn loved Maximilian, but he didn't want to grow old and become his father any more than he wanted to become Oscar Ellington. He wanted Avery to come back to him on her own terms, no one else's.

He wanted her to *choose* him.

She would. She had to. They were meant to be together. Finn knew that as surely as he knew the sun would rise over Montana the next morning, filling Big Sky country with endless rays of hope and light.

Finn needed just a hint of that kind of hope right now. Desperately. Somewhere between Texas and Montana, a bone-deep weariness had come over him. He was too tired to think, too tired to hope, too tired to dream.

He just wanted Avery back in his arms and back in his bed. Until that happened, he was lost. He collapsed fully clothed onto his bed and closed his eyes against a darkness so deep that he felt like he was choking on it. And when sleep finally came, he dreamed of his daughter. He dreamed of Avery and the life the three of them could have together—a life filled with love and joy and as many children and baby goats as Avery wanted. He'd give her anything and everything.

But when he woke up, she wasn't there. Of course she wasn't. It was silly to think she'd chase him back to Montana the moment after he'd left her daddy's mansion. She needed time. Of course she did. But she'd come back—she had to come back. Finn went about his day on autopilot, doing his best to simply get through the hours until Avery returned without breaking down.

For once in his life, Maximilian held his tongue. He must have sensed Finn's need for silence on the matter of his missing wife, because when he strolled into the kitchen to find Finn staring blankly out the big picture window at Pumpkin romping and playing in her new pen, he simply rested a single arm around his shoulder in a tentative one-armed man hug. The unprecedented tenderness of the father-and-son moment caused a lump to lodge firmly in Finn's throat. He nodded, then strode outside to feed the goat to keep the dam of emotions welled up inside him from breaking.

The day wore on, and he busied himself with the daily comfort of ranch work—mending fences, tending to cattle, filling the stalls in the barn with fresh water and hay. His brothers and the ranch hands steered clear, leaving him space and time to brood. In his solitude, Finn worked harder than he had in years, because that's what true cowboys did. They did what needed to be done, no matter what. When they made a promise, they kept it.

He brushed a few stray flakes of hay from his black T-shirt as the air in the barn shifted from soft pink light to the purple shadows of twilight. His back ached, and so did his heart. The day was done, the horses were locked up for the night and the cattle fed, but still there was no sign whatsoever of Avery.

Finn pulled his Stetson low over his eyes and pressed his fist into his lower back, seeking relief. Then, for the first time all day, he allowed himself to consider the possibility that he'd been wrong, that maybe Avery wasn't coming back to the Ambling A. Not today...not ever.

His throat grew thick again, and just like this morning when Maximilian had given him the closest thing to a true embrace they'd ever shared, he felt as if he was on the verge of tears for the first time in his adult life. But then he heard something that gave him pause—an excited little bleat coming from the direction of Pumpkin's pen. Finn's heart stuttered to a stop.

It was silly, really. Baby kids got excited about anything and everything. Just because Pumpkin was suddenly making a ruckus didn't mean the goat's—and

Finn's—favorite person in the world had suddenly reappeared.

But hope welled up in his chest nonetheless. And when he bolted out the barn door and saw Avery's familiar silhouette framed by a perfect autumn sunset, he nearly fell to his knees in relief.

"Avery," he said, his voice rusty and raw. "Thank God."

He held out his arms, but instead of running toward him, Avery slowed to a stop and gave him a watery smile. It was the saddest, most lonely smile he'd ever seen, and that's when Finn knew. He knew it with every desperate beat of his battered heart.

His wife had come home to say goodbye.

The relief in Finn's weary face nearly shattered Avery's resolve.

Clearly he was happy to see her. Elated, even after she'd spent the duration of her travel day—two flights, one three-hour layover and the winding drive to Rust Creek Falls from Billings—convincing herself that she was doing the right thing. The *only* thing. As hard as walking away from Finn would be, it wouldn't be as torturous as building a life with a man who didn't love her, constantly waiting for the shoe to drop and everything she held most dear to crumble to the ground.

She was sure she couldn't do that to herself, and she was positive she couldn't do it to her baby. Better to develop some sort of reasonable, platonic co-parenting arrangement now than end up having to try to find her way once Finn remembered he'd never had any interest in marriage in the first place...to anyone, least of all her.

But she couldn't tell Finn what she needed to say over the phone. He'd been by her side since the moment she'd told him she was pregnant, which was more than she could say for her own flesh and blood. In the end, she'd been the one to run, not him. So he deserved to hear the news face-to-face.

First, though…

She sent a gentle smile to the baby goat bleating excitedly and butting her furry head against the hay bale in the center of her pen. "What is Pumpkin doing here?"

Finn removed his Stetson, raked a hand through his hair and replaced it. Avery tried, and failed, not to stare at the flex of his biceps as he did so. "You said you missed her, so when I went looking for you at the boarding house, I asked Melba and Old Gene if I could bring her to the Ambling A."

Oh. Wow. He'd gone looking for her at the boarding house? "I'm guessing Melba was delighted with that arrangement."

Finn nodded. "She said something about Pumpkin belonging to you already."

Once you name an animal, it's yours.

Avery could hear Melba's voice in her head as clearly as if she were standing right beside her.

How was she going to do this? She loved life in Rust Creek Falls. She loved everything about it.

"I think we should get an annulment," she said without any sort of prelude. If she didn't say it now, she never would. "Or if we don't qualify for one of those, then a divorce."

The *D* word. She barely forced it out. Her voice cracked midway through, turning it into three or four syllables instead of two.

Finn said nothing.

He just stood there staring at her as if she'd kicked him in the stomach. Behind him, the mountains shimmered in shades of red and gold. Never in her life had she thought complete and utter heartbreak could be surrounded by so much beauty.

She cleared her throat and forced herself to finish the speech she'd been mentally rehearsing for hours. "This is all my fault. I take full responsibility. I should have told you about the baby from the very beginning, and I never should have suggested our marriage be one of convenience."

It seemed so absurd now. How could she have ever thought a fake marriage was a good idea when, all along, her feelings for Finn had been heart-stoppingly real?

"It was just..." she continued while nearby, Pumpkin bounced on and off a bale of hay. *It was just the worst mistake I've ever made.* Avery swallowed hard. "It was wrong."

The set of Finn's jaw hardened. His soft brown eyes—eyes that usually danced with laughter and Finn's trademark devilish charm—darkened to black. "*Wrong?*

That's the word you'd use to describe our marriage?"

Avery shook her head. This wasn't going at all how she'd planned. "Please, Finn. You know what I mean."

She was referring to the agreement they'd made not to become intimate, and he knew it. But neither of them could seem to acknowledge it out loud, probably because that arrangement had been nothing short of impossible. She'd fallen into bed with Finn almost instantaneously, and despite all the hurt feelings swirling between them, she still wanted him. She craved the weight of his body on top of hers, the velvety warmth of his skin, his searing kiss. She always would.

"I appreciate everything you were willing to do for me—" she paused for a breath, then forced the rest of the words out "—for the baby. But I should have never agreed to rely on you for money, no matter the circumstances. That's all sorted out now, and I'm not going to hold you to an agreement we never should have made in the first place."

There, it was done. Almost.

Finn deserved to know the whole truth before she walked away for good. "What the baby and I both need isn't money or security. It's love. *Real* love. And I can't let myself settle for a knockoff."

"What the heck are you talking about?" Finn's voice boomed louder than Avery had ever heard it before. It even startled poor Pumpkin into inactivity. She let out a mournful bleat. "Are you crazy? Of course I love you. Why would you think otherwise?"

Avery opened her mouth to yell right back at him, and then blinked, trying to wrap her mind around what he'd just said.

Surely she'd heard him wrong.

"But you…" She shook her head, and hot tears filled her eyes.

He couldn't be serious, but Avery didn't think he'd toy with her emotions. Not at a time like this. Finn had never once told her he loved her, though. How was she supposed to know?

"I love you, Avery! I fell in love with you the first night we were together back in Oklahoma!" He yelled it so loud that there was no way she could misunderstand. The entire population of Rust Creek Falls probably knew Finn Crawford loved her now.

Avery didn't know how to process it, though. It was too much, more than her fragile heart could handle after all she'd been through in recent weeks.

She burst into tears.

"Don't cry, love," Finn said, closing the distance between them and taking her into his arms. "I'm sorry for yelling. It's just that I've been tied up in knots, worried you weren't coming back."

He pressed a tender kiss to the top of

her head as she buried her face in his shoulder. He smelled like hay and horses, farm and family...like all the things she'd come to love so much about life here in this wild, beautiful place.

"I love you," he said, gently this time. Like a whisper.

Avery closed her eyes, wanting to believe, but needing to be sure. What if this was still just about the baby?

She shook her head against the soft fabric of his T-shirt, fighting as hard as she could. But falling for Finn Crawford had always been as easy and sweet as falling onto a feather bed.

"You love me, or the baby?" she managed to murmur, even as she felt her heart beating hard in perfect harmony against his.

Finn pulled away slightly, took her face in his hands and forced her to meet his gaze. "I love both of you, Princess. I'll admit it threw me when you told me you were pregnant, and I definitely could have handled the news better. Our relationship hasn't exactly been traditional."

He sighed, and the corner of his mouth tugged into a familiar half smile.

Had Rust Creek Falls' most notoriously single Crawford just used the word *relationship*?

"But, darlin', there was always a part of me that connected with you right from the start. Didn't you feel it, too, Princess?" His gaze dropped to her mouth as the pad of his thumb brushed a tender trail along her bottom lip. "Don't you feel it now?"

Then her husband dipped his head and kissed her as the sun fell on another autumnal day in Montana, and while the horses whinnied in the barn and the trees on the horizon blazed ruby red, the last bit of Avery's resistance faded away.

She felt it, too—with every breath,

every kiss, every captivated beat of her heart. She felt it.

This kiss, this place…this man she loved so much. Finn Crawford wasn't just the father of her baby. He was her home, and at long last, Avery Ellington Crawford was home to stay.

Epilogue

Hours later, Avery lay in Finn's bed, naked and sated. Once again, he'd scooped her off her feet and carried her upstairs, where he'd made love to her in the same bed where she'd somehow managed to convince herself that he didn't love her.

How could she have been so wrong?

The question nagged at her in the afterglow. Finn had told her why he'd been going on so many dates. He'd even admitted he hadn't slept with anyone since their night together in Oklahoma. How had she taken the beautiful moment when he'd kissed her belly and whispered *mine* as something else—something frightening and lonely? Something to run away from.

She wondered if the answer was somehow tangled up in the ugly episode of her disinheritance. She thought maybe so, but she didn't want to think about that now. She'd made peace with her father, and in the end, her mother had stood up for her in a way she never could have imagined. On some level, she was glad it had happened. Being cut off from her family had taught her some important truths. It taught her she was capable of standing on her own two feet and making her own decisions. It taught her what kind of parent she wanted to be to her baby. And most of all, it taught her she could trust Finn Crawford. He was a keeper, and she had no intention of running again. Ever.

He ran tender fingertips across her baby bump, then pressed a hand to her heart and whispered her favorite word.

"Mine."

Her heart was his, now and forever. Past, present and always.

"I have an idea," he said, shooting her one of his boyish grins.

"Oh, yeah? Does this idea involve a goat?" She kind of wanted another one. Another baby, too, now that she was thinking about it. The more, the merrier. After all, the Ambling A had plenty of room.

"It does not." He arched a brow. "Unless you want Pumpkin to be part of our wedding. That could be arranged. Maybe she could be the ring bearer. Don't people do that with dogs?"

Avery shifted so she could get a better look at his expression. Was he serious?

"Aren't you forgetting something, cowboy? We're already married."

He picked up her hand and toyed with the rose gold band on her finger. Someday Avery might pass it on to their daughter and tell her the story of how she'd married her father in tiny country courthouse in Great Gulch where the bailiff wore spurs. And then maybe her daughter would pass it on to her own child, and so on and so on, so that generations of Crawfords would remember the fine man who'd won her heart against all odds.

"I know we're already married, but I'd like to have another wedding—a ceremony like the one Wren asked you about. A big celebration that both our families could attend." He bent to kiss her, warm and tender. "Think about it. How does that sound, Princess?"

She smiled at her husband. She didn't

need to think about anything. The answer fell right off her tongue. "Perfect."

Just like a fairy tale.

* * * * *